Leather and Grit

ROPING IN HIS HEART

JON KEYS

Roping in His Heart
ISBN # 978-1-83943-804-2
©Copyright Jon Keys 2019
Cover Art by Erin Dameron-Hill ©Copyright September 2019
Interior text design by Claire Siemaszkiewicz
Pride Publishing

ROPING IN HIS HEART

Chapter One

Dakota groaned and shifted his position so the bright morning sunshine fell onto the bare body beside him. He lifted himself to his elbow and studied the pile of naked men spread across the bed he usually shared only with Ayden. The other two were buckle buddies they'd picked up the previous night. His guess would put them a good five years younger than either him or Ayden. They were college hustlers trolling for a cowboy to satisfy the itch they had for rodeo dick. One of them stretched and turned so his smooth, pale ass slid closer to Dakota. He extended his hand to caress the twink's butt. When the young man whined and wiggled nearer, Dakota decided one night with these two filled any kind of wild-oats-sowing he'd needed.

As he worked his way off the bed, the faint banging of pots and pans in use drifted into the bedroom. *Ayden. I should have guessed he'd make breakfast. He's always such a do-gooder.* Then the aroma of fresh coffee and frying bacon reached him, and Dakota's focus changed to the cooking odors he smelled. He swung his feet onto the plush hotel carpet. With clothes scattered across the room, he decided digging for underwear sounded like something he'd like to avoid. Certain the other two wouldn't be waking soon, he slipped into the living area buck naked.

He strolled across the white rug to stand in front of the floor-to-ceiling window and enjoy the warmth of the morning sunshine. A few seconds later, he stretched and tugged at his balls as he took in the sight of the giant steel-and-glass buildings surrounding him.

"You better watch who you're giving a show to. This isn't Vegas."

With a chuckle, Dakota slipped behind Ayden, drew him into a tight hug and kissed the side of his neck.

"Morning, babe. How are you? Did you enjoy yourself last night?" Dakota asked as he let his hands slip down Ayden's chest.

Ayden squirmed in his arms, chuckling as he grabbed Dakota's wrists and tugged him away. "Stop! You know how ticklish I am."

Dakota ran his fingers through the thick patch of hair surrounding Ayden's good bits then pulled his hands higher, exploring Ayden's chest before planting another kiss. Ayden laughed again as he dodged Dakota's embrace and went to the small refrigerator they'd stocked when they'd arrived. He waved Dakota toward the full pot of coffee as he checked the fridge. "The coffee's finished. Get some before our guests come out of their comas."

Dakota searched the kitchen cabinets, pulled out two white coffee mugs and poured them almost full. He stepped to the icebox and swatted Ayden's bare ass as his boyfriend picked out a few more things for breakfast.

Ayden snickered and glanced back at Dakota. "You better be careful or your sunny-side eggs will be well done."

Dakota put a few drops of half-and-half into his mug then finished filling Ayden's cup with cream and sugar. He set the swirling mixture beside Ayden, put his stout brew on the counter and hoisted himself up beside it. As he took his first sip, Ayden motioned in his direction. "You're kind of close to where I'm cooking. I'd hate to get bacon grease splattered on your family jewels. I don't know if you could go without sex long enough for it to heal."

Dakota studied Ayden while he took a drink of coffee, enjoying the warm sensation as it washed through his system. Once he'd swallowed, he refocused and blew Ayden a kiss. "You're the one with his willie a few inches from hot grease. Besides, if I get burns, you'll have to kiss them and make them all better."

"One of these days someone is going to get more attention than you," Ayden said with a laugh.

Dakota shook his head. "Nope, not going to happen." He stole a piece of crisp bacon from the platter and winked as he bit off the end.

Ayden laid another few pieces of thick bacon in the skillet to fry. Then he pushed a loaf of fresh sourdough toward Dakota and pointed to the knives along the tiled backsplash. "Make yourself useful and slice the bread."

"No problem, boss. But I'm telling you those two aren't going to be awake for at least a couple of hours."

Ayden waved a hand toward Dakota. "Just do it."

Dakota shrugged and carved the bread into Texas-size slices. Once he'd finished, there were several stacks of bread on the cutting board. He knew what Ayden had in mind and coated each slice with a generous amount of butter, first one side then the other. As Ayden cracked a half-dozen eggs into the sizzling hot bacon drippings, Dakota heated a sauté pan and laid slices of buttered bread on its hot surface. In a few minutes, he added a platter of buttered toast to the feast Ayden had created.

They seated themselves at the glass dining table and Dakota wiggled before grinning. "These chairs are gonna leave me with waffle butt."

Ayden studied Dakota's bare ass cheek through the glass and grinned. "True. You're going to have decorations, but it's still a fine ass."

About the time Dakota finished filling his plate, there was a crash, followed by a few select profanities from the bedroom. He lifted an eyebrow. "Sounds like our guests are up."

Another bang followed by a chorus of cursing drifted through the suite.

"Well, they're working on waking up at least."

Ayden pushed back his chair but Dakota stopped him. "They think they're adults. Let them figure out what to do."

Ayden drew his lips into a thin line but, after listening for a moment, he turned back to the meal. When Dakota snorted, Ayden paused halfway to his mouth with a fork filled with breakfast. "We don't want the food to get cold."

"That's it. I'm worried about the eggs getting cold. Yup, the eggs might get a chill."

Ayden paused and gave Dakota a glare, which turned into a grin. "Shut up or you can cook for the next month."

About the time Dakota had finished miming locking his lips and throwing away the key, the first of their overnight guests stumbled into the room. He mimicked a vampire's reaction when light hit them — at least the way they did in every bad vamp movie Dakota had ever seen. The college kid turned away, yanked up his jeans and buttoned them closed. When he turned back to the pair enjoying their quiet breakfast, he continued to shade his eyes from the morning sun.

"Fuck. Can't you close the damn curtain? It's too fucking sunny in here."

Dakota kept his typical smart-ass comments from coloring his next words as he pointed to the carafe filled with pitch-black liquid. "Ayden's made coffee. Grab yourself a cup if you'd like. There's breakfast on the counter too."

The pause stretched out while Dakota dug into his meal. Then he realized Ayden's chuckle had grown louder. He slowed to a stop and caught Ayden's scrutiny.

"What?" Dakota asked.

Ayden cut his eyes toward the half-clothed twenty-something. When Dakota followed Ayden's gaze, he saw the kid staring at Dakota's naked body. He let the exhibition go a little longer before calling him on it.

"See anything you like?"

"I think he's more ready for a breakfast sausage than thick-cut bacon," Ayden said.

"I see one thing I'd like to get more of," the college student said.

The last of the words had barely left his mouth when the other half of the pair stumbled in, tugging at the zipper on his jeans. He paused for a moment, taking in the scene. He curled his lips into a grin and winked at his friend. "Kev, why didn't you wake me?"

Kev had made his way to the kitchenette and filled his plate. As he shoveled food into his mouth, he wagged his fork. "I tried to get your fat ass up. You made weird noises and put the pillow over your head."

Ayden sighed and finished the last of the food on his plate. As he drained his coffee, he caught Dakota's eye. "I'll let the three of you enjoy the rest of breakfast. Eat whatever you want. Check-out time is ten."

Ayden took his dishes and put them on the kitchen counter, giving Dakota a chance to admire his hot body. When Dakota turned back, it was to glances that reminded him of hungry hens after a fat grasshopper. He had no desire to be the meal for these two, so he put his fork to use and enjoyed the last of his food. Once he'd taken care of his plate, he turned back to the pair, just in time to catch them with their eyes locked on his crotch. He decided a little teasing wouldn't be out of line. If they were going to stare, he'd give them something to remember.

He smirked as he studied them then seated himself on the counter. He eased his legs farther apart until his goods were displayed across the stone surface. Dakota decided that he'd sat on more comfortable things, but once he saw their faces, he was willing to tolerate some chill to drag these two into their own special brand of cowboy fantasy. They reminded Dakota of his dad's Blue Heelers begging for leftovers from the table. When he thought about it, they were after meat, the same as the pups. The similarity put a grin on his face.

"Last night was fun. Hope y'all enjoyed it as much as we did." Dakota teased the hair around his navel until they wiped sweat off their faces and licked their lips.

Then he let his hand slip lower until he ran the tips of his fingers through his dark pubic hair. After a few minutes of teasing and when the two victims were seconds from popping in their pants, he stretched his tube of foreskin between his fingers, toyed with it for a moment then jumped to the floor. One of them moaned — Dakota didn't know which — but he had them at the level he'd wanted.

"Well, boys, I guess it's about time to clean up and get back to the rodeo. I'll catch up with Ayden. We'll see you in a bit." With a smile straight out of the legends of Coyote, he strolled from the room. By the time he reached the bedroom, the sounds coming from the living room left no doubt what was happening. He opened the door to find Ayden drying himself with a giant towel as thick as the carpet. As he dried between his legs, he glanced at Dakota with a smirk.

"Did you get them amped?"

Dakota put his finger to his lips, signaling Ayden to silence. It didn't take long for a symphony of moans and the slap of taut skin to fill the rooms. They listened for a few moments before Dakota grinned. "Sounds like something — or some*body* — got them all worked up."

Ayden tossed the towel into the bathroom, wrapped his fist around Dakota's cock and squeezed. "Oh yeah. I can't imagine what has them so excited." He released Dakota, aimed him toward the bathroom and swatted him on the butt. "Go wash off your crusty junk. By the time you're done, the two in the other room will be finished."

A guttural moan filled the suite.

"Or they may be done sooner. But get your ass in gear. We've spent enough time with this pair."

Dakota gave Ayden a tender kiss then strolled into the bathroom, making certain to work his butt so Ayden got a nice display. As he turned on the shower, he felt a presence in there with him. Dakota turned toward the door as he tested the temperature of the water with his hand. Ayden trailed into the shower behind him. With the spray from multiple heads hitting them from all sides, he ran his hands over the wet hair covering Dakota's chest. When Ayden dug his nails into Dakota's sensitive nipples, sparks of pleasure flooded his body.

He growled at Ayden. "You're getting something started."

"Which was my intent. It wasn't just the youngsters who got excited by the sight of your cock at breakfast."

"The calf roping doesn't start for hours. I wouldn't mind some fun before checkout."

Ayden sank to his knees and grabbed Dakota's butt before taking his hardening shaft between his lips. The heat of Ayden's mouth enveloped Dakota's dick as he took his boyfriend's hair in his hands and thrust. Ayden's tight throat drove Dakota toward his orgasm. The warm spray from a handful of shower nozzles only added to the experience.

"I'm close, and it's a big fucking load. You better pull off…"

When Ayden showed no sign of slowing, Dakota twisted his fingers through the wet ringlets covering Ayden's head and started a face fucking that left both of them groaning in appreciation.

The oh-so-familiar pleasure built in his crotch. As the intensity grew, Dakota's cock throbbed from Ayden's attention. It didn't take much before the first tidal wave of orgasm crashed over him. A low groan came from his lips as he unloaded into Ayden's throat. Once the last ripple of ecstasy had ebbed, Dakota helped Ayden to his feet and shared a scorching kiss. As he intertwined their tongues, Dakota enjoyed the delightful tastes. But as they held each other, Ayden's hard shaft slid across Dakota's stomach.

Without a word, Dakota squatted in front of Ayden and appreciated the sight before him. Ayden's dark brown hair was repeated in the groomed strip running between his pecs to the bush from which his rigid cock jutted. Dakota wrapped his hand around Ayden's dick and tugged back his ample foreskin. After a few slow strokes, he slid close and slipped his tongue into Ayden's hood.

The tastes and scents he found inside had become a favorite treat each time they made love. He explored Ayden's cock for several satisfying minutes before shifting his attention. He moved to the twin goose eggs Ayden carried for a set of balls. As he cradled them in his hand, Dakota pulled their sac lower until a bass rumble came from Ayden.

A few seconds later, Ayden groaned, "Damn, that's excellent. I love when you tease my balls."

Dakota sucked one in. As he coated it with spit, Ayden trembled and Dakota knew he had pushed too far.

"Ah, fuck. I'm coming!"

The shaking grew as Ayden grabbed Dakota's shorn head. A cry of pleasure marked the beginning of Ayden's climax. Dakota quickly swallowed Ayden's dick just as cum flooded his mouth until it dribbled from the corner. He took the last volleys and savored the bittersweet taste. When Ayden gave a final sigh, his softening cock slipped from between Dakota's lips.

He stood, held Ayden tight and gave him a lingering kiss before tugging them back under the warm spray. They rinsed and were soon using the last of the plush towels to dry themselves. As he slipped on a pair of deep red boxer briefs, voices from the other room drifted over to them. He glanced toward Ayden with a chuckle. "I think the bunnies are done. We need to get packed and back to the rodeo grounds."

Ayden nodded in agreement as he pulled clothes from the suitcase.

Chapter Two

Dakota wiped his sleeve over his forehead, drying the sweat gathering there before he settled the cowboy hat into place. He took a deep breath then let it leak out, calming himself. His horse had a bushel of tricks that kept both of them on edge, not that he presented a particular challenge to ride. Jack was a gelding on trial from a trainer in West Texas, which meant if there were too many issues, he'd just try the next mount in the rotation. Dakota had been on horseback ever since he could remember. He'd grown up on his parents' ranch close to the Black Hills, which sometimes seemed a world away from the acreage he and Ayden had bought a few years back. Dakota had argued for a place to call their own. Building the arena had been the first thing on his wish list.

While I had the dream, I couldn't put two boards on top of each other without them falling apart. Ayden has mad skills and his welding talent saved the day. Ayden has the knowhow and I have the muscle. He was a skilled craftsman, and I had no problem being his helper. As a result, they'd built one of the finest practice arenas Dakota had ever seen, and easy access to a well-designed facility had improved the roping times for both of them.

His mount tucked his head and popped his hindquarters upward into a stunt Dakota recognized as his version of impatience. The gelding was far too much of a gentleman to buck, but he had enough fire in his belly to let Dakota know when he got bored...and he'd been still while they'd planned the practice session. His breeding and training weren't to prepare him to stand beside a pen of prime roping calves. Dakota hadn't worked out all of his shenanigans yet, but he did this one often enough that Dakota recognized it – and knew the solution. He turned to Ayden, "He's getting antsy. I'm going to trot him a few rounds. That'll work out some of his nervousness."

"Yeah, I wondered." He winked at Dakota. "Take him out. I'll still be here."

Dakota leaned over to tussle Ayden's hair before sending Jack into a sprint. Without looking, he knew Ayden would wear an expression of aggravation while he worked to get his hair in order. The mental image stretched a smile across Dakota's face.

Jack reached the conclusion of his gallop at the opposite end of the pen. Before making a return sprint, a commotion coming from the direction of the county road grabbed his attention.

Dakota glanced toward the ranch entrance when the rattle of a pickup signaled a guest to their home. He reined Jack to a stop beside Ayden and his mount as they waited to see who had found their way down the isolated country road.

It had been their intention to make their headquarters remote, which meant that whoever this was had made an effort to find them. By the time the truck had rolled to a stop, a smile erupted across Dakota's face. He knew the visitors. He'd recognized them as Shane Rees and his husband, Dustin. Jack had been raised on Shane's ranch, and Shane had trained him. The truck doors popped open and Shane stepped from the pickup with a wave.

"Hey, Dakota. How are things going?" Shane said.

"Not bad. Just working with Jack."

Shane took a few quick steps and vaulted the pipe fence. He cleared the top with no trouble, and with a few strides of his long legs, he stood beside the gelding.

With an acknowledgment from Dakota, he went over the animal with a fine-toothed comb. At some point in the examination, Dakota decided it would be easier for all of them if he wasn't mounted on Jack. He held the reins as Shane checked him with more attention to detail.

"Don't think nothing about Shane checking him so closely. Jack got treated more like a pet than a roping horse."

Dakota turned to find that Dustin had made his way across the pen but he didn't mind. Dakota had always felt comfortable around Shane's husband. His sense of humor was one Dakota could appreciate. He nodded toward Dustin and winked at the whipcord-lean bull rider.

He'd met the couple a few years earlier and the four of them had hit it off. It had happened at the beginning of the friendship between him and Ayden. They'd found it helpful to have another gay couple to spend time with, since they had a lot in common — not everything, but enough so they maintained a comfortable relationship.

Shane lifted one of the gelding's front legs and checked it before moving to the next hoof, which he gave a similar amount of scrutiny. Dakota turned to see if Dustin could tell him what was happening, but he began a running explanation before Dakota could form questions.

"He does this. His family is crazy about their quarter horses. Since Jack is one he trained... Well, it goes a long way beyond being proud of the breeding lines. Some days I think he gives his animals more attention than he does Austin."

Shane appeared from around the horse's front shoulder. "I give Austin plenty of love. He's the next generation, after all. We're counting on him to continue the ranch."

Shane disappeared around the horse again, and Dakota considered what Shane said before asking. "Who's Austin?"

His question seemed to delight Dustin. "Austin is our five-year-old nephew, who is the apple of the entire Rees family's eye."

"We aren't that bad," Shane said from the opposite side of the horse.

"Oh, please," Dustin said with a wink toward Dakota. "The boots you bought him cost double what mine did."

Shane ducked under the horse's neck, patting him on the shoulder. "He's in great shape. Looks like you've taken good care of him." He lifted an eyebrow toward Dustin. "Austin is *not* spoiled. His boots are more expensive because he has better taste than you do. Besides, his are dress boots."

Dustin snorted but added no more to the conversation. Dakota studied them before remounting the horse. With a nudge of his knee, Jack spun in place. Another touch sent him turning the opposite direction for a revolution.

Shane climbed the fence opposite Dakota and motioned toward the open arena. "Seems like you have him working some new tricks. Why don't we run a few calves past him?"

Dakota calmed Jack with a few familiar maneuvers then backed him into the roping box while Ayden readied the calf. Dakota signaled the release with a quick nod of his head.

The red-and-white speckled calf rocketed from the chute and sprinted toward the opposite end of the enclosure as if wolves were chasing it. A split-second later, Jack jumped into pursuit with enough power to impress his rider. Dakota flicked the rope over his head until the lariat gained a life of its own and he shot the loop forward.

Jack dug his hooves into the loose dust just as the calf hit the end of the rope. Dakota vaulted from his back and ran down the lariat to throw the calf. Once he'd grabbed three of the calf's legs, he flipped his pigging string around the squirming bovine's shins three times before a final flip secured the tie and Dakota threw his hands into the air.

Ayden called out the time. He stood, brushing the dust from his jeans.

"Well, fuck. That sucks. My grandma could beat that time," Dakota said.

Dustin turned the stopwatch so he could read it. "Twelve-point-two. That's pretty good."

Dakota mounted then rode back to the small group, his face in a grimace. "The top ropers at Nationals are way below ten seconds."

Shane studied them before turning his gaze to Dakota. "It was a respectable run. The top cowboys in last year's National Finals were in the eight-second range. You're close."

Dakota considered the comments as he leaned down to pat the horse's shoulder. He twisted his mouth then he replied. "I guess I've only been working with him for a month. When the ride goes well, we place in the money."

Shane nodded. "He's got heart. The more time you spend with him, the better he will get."

Dakota studied Shane and Dustin before dismounting, considering the cowboy's advice. Before he replied, a small red pickup shot into the driveway, fishtailing before coming to a stop beside the other vehicles. A groan escaped Ayden, and Dakota raised his eyebrows. Dustin glanced at each of them then chuckled.

"Someone you know?" Dustin asked.

"My ex-wife..." Dakota said.

Dustin looked first at him then Ayden, but Dakota wasn't going to explain Kayla. He got the same mixed emotions every time he dealt with his former wife. They hadn't been together for several years, but the lapsed days didn't make her visits any more comfortable. But he and Kayla worked to maintain their friendship, which extended all the way back to high school.

We were always better friends than lovers. I'm glad we've been able to stay friends.

She started toward him, stopping when a high-pitched voice came from the back seat.

"Mama, let me out. I wanna see Dakota too!"

That was Rory. Whatever she wanted would not have a quick resolution. Dakota rode Jack to the fence, dismounted and handed the reins to his boyfriend. Their eyes met, and Dakota could see the resignation. He knew Ayden would rather not share their life with Kayla and Rory, but there were things he considered his responsibility. While it frustrated him to deal with them, Rory and Kayla belonged in the group of individuals he made time for in his life.

"Mama! I want out."

Kayla rolled her eyes and turned back to the vehicle. A few seconds later, a miniature cowboy in the guise of a five-year-old climbed from the truck. From the deep red boots to the cowboy hat complete with stampede string, the child walking toward him was trying hard to pull off the appearance of a hardened ranch hand.

Rory had become one of his main points of contention with Kayla. The youngster had resulted from a brief relationship she'd had after their divorce. Regardless of his pedigree, the pint-sized force of will had worked his way into Dakota's heart. It frustrated him that Kayla hadn't chased after the biological father with the same tenacity she had him. Regardless, he had a huge soft spot for Rory. Dakota had been an only child and liked getting his own way with almost everything.

His silent tirade came to a halt when the kid ran at him with his arms spread wide. "Dakota!"

Rory's demonstration of unadulterated love washed over him and his typically self-serving attitude evaporated. Dakota grabbed the youngster and swung him around as Rory giggled. After a few spins, he set the boy down and gave him a smile before introducing him. "Everyone, this is Rory. He's a buddy of mine from way back."

Rory scanned the small crowd and shot everyone a grin. "Hey, y'all. I'm Dakota's roping buddy. We're gettin' ready for National Finals. We're gonna whip their asses and take home the winnings."

Dakota reached down and tipped Rory's hat so it covered the top of his face. "What did we say about using adult talk?"

The boy's gaze dropped and he dug the toe of his boot into the hard-packed dirt while his face turned the color of a ripe tomato. "You said I was too little. You said if I use bad words we can't be rodeo buddies no more."

Dakota softened as tears grew in the corners of Rory's eyes. He couldn't stand to upset the youngster. Kayla had told him before how much the boy treasured his time with Dakota. When the dejected form standing in front of him shook, he broke.

Dakota patted the youngster's back. "Buck up, buckaroo. We'll always be buddies. You don't worry about that. But watch it with the bad words." He leaned closer to Rory and said in a lower tone, "Your mom might not let you come back if you say them." Rory turned with a giant sniff, wiped his eyes on his sleeve and met Dakota's gaze.

"You sure?"

The last of the chill left Dakota's heart. "Of course I'm sure. You'll always be my main helper."

The beginnings of a grin appeared on Rory's lips. "Can I pet Jack?"

"Sure. But stay around his head. I don't want you to get kicked."

"I'll be careful!"

Rory ran toward the gelding, shot through the pipe fence and was soon giving him all the affection he could muster. The horse gained energy from the youngster and clearly enjoyed his time with the fearless little person. Several minutes passed before Dakota felt comfortable that Rory would be safe with the horse. He took a deep breath before turning to find out why Kayla had made the trip to see him. He figured it was another case of her needing a sitter for Rory, but he knew better than to second guess her motives. Their relationship had always been...complicated. He couldn't hope for this time to be different, and from her expression, it might even be worse than he envisioned. He braced himself, hoping he was ready to deal with whatever issue had brought her out.

"Hey, Kayla. What's up?"

As he expected, she plunged in with no hesitation. "I have a new job at a big distribution center out of state. I was hoping you'd change the alimony without us needing to go back to court." She paused and glanced at Rory before continuing. "I don't want to stress the kid out with a whole drawn-out issue. It will be enough when he realizes he won't get to see you and Ayden."

Dakota studied her as he worked to reach a solution to the problem she had presented. Ayden had already clued in on Dakota's need for privacy and had left to give Shane and Dustin a tour of the farm. The peacock Ayden had acquired from a neighbor began its call, which was loud enough to cover any conversation between the two of them.

He refocused on his ex-wife, hoping they could work out an arrangement without earth-bending drama. Once he reached his decision, Dakota outlined his conditions.

"Because of Rory, I'll keep paying the alimony. But he has a daddy, and that guy needs to be supporting him. That would be the minimum I think he owes the kid, but those issues are between you and the deadbeat — not me."

Kayla started to argue but stopped when Dakota held up a hand to silence her.

"Let me finish. I also don't want Rory to think I've disappeared. So, I want visitation whenever you come back — and I'm not talking about an hour or something like that."

"You know my mom hates you. She has a fit every time I bring him to see you," Kayla said.

Dakota shrugged. "Your mother never liked me, so I don't know how this would change anything. Either I see Rory or we can take this all back to court. If we go that route, you might get no money at all."

Kayla went rigid, and Dakota knew he'd hit on the issue she'd hoped to avoid. After a few seconds, she nodded. "Okay. I'll make it work. Mom's going to be pissed off, though."

Dakota shrugged. "Not my problem. Was there anything else?"

Kayla had the good grace to hesitate in embarrassment before she continued. "Could you keep Rory for a bit? I need to get things ready for the trip and it would be faster without him under foot."

Dakota felt something close to relief at hearing an offer that felt more typical, a request that wasn't life changing. With a shrug, he addressed Kayla's request. "Ayden and I planned to work with the new roping horse. I'm sure the two of us can keep an eye on Rory while we do."

"Keep him busy and he'll take a nap after lunch," Kayla said.

This time Dakota couldn't keep from rolling his eyes. "Goody. He can go down with Ayden."

"What is Ayden going down with?"

Dakota turned to discover his boyfriend had returned from touring the ranch with Shane and Dustin. At this moment, he looked unhappy. Those expressions usually meant Dakota was in trouble. He plastered on a toothy smile before working to bail out his butt. "Rory is going to hang with us today while Kayla runs a few errands. I was just pointing out that the two of you might nap together."

The silence dragged on as Ayden glared at Dakota. Dustin grabbed Shane by the arm and guided him toward their truck. He put on a smile. "Nice to see everybody. I think we're ready to work with Jack this week. We'll talk to you later."

The shit hit the fan at that point, and before Dakota knew what happened, Ayden had taken Rory away to gather eggs, which he loved to do, and Dustin and Shane had gone. He was alone with Kayla to discuss the issue. He sighed and turned his full attention toward her.

Before Dakota could say anything, Kayla grabbed him in a hug that lasted long enough for Dakota to feel awkward. About that time, she released him and patted his cheek. "I'm hoping this will give Rory and me a life of our own. We can't stay with my folks anymore."

Dakota studied her before he heard Rory's laughter, which made his final decision easy. "We'll help you any way we can. We like it when Rory visits. You've had a rough time the last few years. I'm sure everything will turn out the way you want."

Kayla gave him another quick embrace before letting him go. "Thank you. It will be amazing—and yes, I will bring him to see you whenever we come back to visit. I want Rory to know you and Ayden. Y'all are an important part of our lives."

There was a loud squawk from the direction the youngster had taken. This time Dakota laughed. "You should haul it out of here. That was the rooster, and it sounds like Rory thinks it would be a good idea to show him who's boss."

Kayla made her way to her pickup and climbed inside. As she drove past, she gave Dakota a last wave.

He watched until she was out of sight before strolling over to see what had happened with Rory and Ayden on their adventure. His thoughts began to turn maudlin until the combination of a war-whoop from Rory, a yell of warning from Ayden and a cry from the chicken yard sent Dakota running to the rescue — but he wasn't sure whose.

Chapter Three

Ayden held on to Rory's hand, still uncertain how he had gotten involved in this family outing, when none of the people in the group were his relatives.

Some of them I don't even like.

But he knew why he'd been roped into doing this. *Dakota.* His boyfriend had claimed to have forgotten about the flea market trip and had made appointments he couldn't cancel. He'd told Ayden in the past that Kayla's mother tolerated him only when it let her and Kayla go shopping. But when he'd met the trio and explained that the arrangements had changed, the women had agreed to allow Ayden to become Dakota's replacement for the family outing. He could have told them no, but he couldn't stand disappointing Rory. Dakota would pay for this later, but for now he would deal with sitter duty. They had been going through the flea market for several hours now, and Ayden knew his little partner had reached the limit of his tolerance for this kind of activity.

Rory snuggled his face against Ayden's muscular shoulder and soon his eyes were closed while he chewed at his thumb. They continued through the acres of sellers scattered through the clumps of leafy post oak and long pole barns constructed of timber and corrugated steel.

A half-hour later, Ayden was still following Kayla and her mother. While he enjoyed these trips when he made them with Dakota, the same event with a young kid and two women who had conned him into being their childcare was not his idea of a fun outing.

Rory squirmed in his arms, bringing Ayden back to the slog. A few steps later, Rory awakened and his ice-blue gaze locked on Ayden.

"Hi," Rory said softly.

Ayden tried not to let his frustration wash onto Rory. "Hey, kiddo. You awake?"

"Yeah…" He hesitated before continuing. "I'm gettin' hungry, and…" This time the hesitation was even longer, to the point that it irritated Ayden. When he explained, Ayden understood. "I gotta pee. Really bad."

Ayden tried to help out Dakota when he could, but taking his ex-wife's son to the nasty flea market port-a-john fell far past his limits. "Kayla, Rory needs to go to the bathroom."

Kayla glanced over from the table of T-shirts. "Could you take him? The bathroom's right there."

Ayden followed the direction she'd motioned. The sight of the bright blue plastic port-a-john was enough to cause him to gag at the thought of going inside the rancid public toilet. This wasn't a line he would cross. He wasn't the parent. This fell under Kayla's responsibility. Ayden lifted Rory from his hip, set him on the ground and walked him over to Kayla. He transferred Rory's grip to his mother. She regarded him with a smile. "I'll buy you lunch if you'll take him."

"Not even for grilled sirloin."

Kayla shrugged and led Rory to the toilet. Just before closing the door behind them, she stuck her tongue out at Ayden then disappeared from sight.

"Men... Y'all are useless."

Ayden turned to Kayla's mother. "Excuse me?"

"You heard me. You could have taken the boy to the bathroom. Suck it up."

Ayden cocked an eyebrow and stared at the older woman. "Linda, Rory's a sweet kid, but he's not mine and he's not my boyfriend's. Why didn't you volunteer to take him if it was such a big deal?"

Her expression twisted and Ayden steeled himself for the expected tirade. As she got ready to unleash her tongue, the toilet door shot open and Rory ran to Ayden and grabbed his hand. He glanced down to find the boy grinning.

"I'm back, Ayden. We can go check out the animals if you want. Momma said you like the pets, especially the birds."

He studied Rory for a few seconds before turning to Kayla. "Actually, I do like birds. All different kinds, even the chickens at the farm."

A serious expression appeared on Rory's face. "Except the rooster. Sometimes he's mean."

Ayden nodded. "I don't think he intends to be mean. He's protecting his hens."

Rory stared at Ayden with an expression of disbelief. When Ayden saw the youngster's face, he couldn't keep from laughing. Still chuckling, he headed toward the section of the flea market reserved for the animal vendors. He followed Rory's lead for several steps before coming to a stop. He turned to Kayla and lifted an eyebrow. "Don't think you got away with anything. I'm watching you."

Her snicker had Ayden rolling his eyes but he didn't want to have their banter turn into something else.

"Ayden, come on! I want to see the birds. What kinds do they have?"

He let Rory lead him into the myriad of walkways, pens and cages. They hadn't traveled far when Rory brought him to an abrupt stop. Ayden looked around, trying to figure out what had attracted the youngster. He realized that with so many animals around them, it was impossible to figure out what had grabbed Rory's attention.

"What's up, guy? What do you see?"

He pointed to a box Ayden had missed. Inside its confines was a lone, male golden pheasant. Ayden had to agree with Rory's assessment. He hadn't seen many animals as striking. When he checked on the boy, his expression was nothing short of rapture. He held out a shaking finger and said in a reverent whisper, "Look, Ayden. It's beautiful."

Ayden worked at being the hard-hearted adult, but one glance at Rory's expression told him he would fail. He lifted the youngster so he could see the bird more clearly. Only a short time passed before Rory reached out to touch the bird.

He gently caught Rory's hand. "Hang on, little guy. It might peck you, and we don't want that."

Rory tensed for a moment then sagged against Ayden. "Okay. It sure is pretty though."

"You're right. It's beautiful. I don't think we'll find another bird like that one. But it's fun to try, isn't it?" He lowered Rory to the pathway and they walked deeper into the market. Any unique bird resulted in at least a brief stop to check it out in more detail. For Rory, everything but chickens fell into the category of amazing. And even some chickens were included.

Ayden didn't mind. He shared Rory's obsession over birds. He'd been drawing plans for the aviary he wanted at the farm. Nothing elaborate, something they could knock out in a weekend. There were birds he'd like to raise, and he might find some today. So, he didn't have an objection when Rory brought their progress to a standstill. They stood for a moment and he heard cooing.

"Ayden, pigeons."

He lowered himself beside Rory to see this latest find. The birds scurried over the pen, eating the grains scattered inside. After he studied them, he realized there were several kinds of pigeons divided into separate compartments. Some he recognized, such as the fantails, which had the appearance of miniature peacocks when their tails spread wide. Most of the types he didn't know. He slipped his finger through the wire mesh and soon had several of the inquisitive birds inspecting him.

"Those are Homers. They used them to send messages for thousands of years. They're pretty impressive birds."

Ayden saw the grizzled face of a man close to three times his age giving him a toothy grin. Before Ayden could ask anything, Rory chimed in with a question. "You have some cool pigeons. Do those really deliver notes?"

The focus of both adults changed to the inquisitive child. The man who had started the conversation paused then addressed Rory. "Homing pigeons will, but not most pigeons. Some don't fly well at all, like the tumblers." He gestured toward the strutting birds before shifting his gaze to Rory. "But the Homers are sleek and speedy. They can find their way home from a hundred miles or more. And they're fast too. Really fast."

Rory locked on one part of the man's narrative. "A hundred miles? Really? Wow."

The man's smile broadened. He'd probably reached the conclusion he would make a sale soon.

"Yes, a hundred miles. You put a little suitcase on his leg, and people sent messages to each other with them."

Ayden fought to keep from laughing as Rory swallowed hard and turned to him. "Wow, isn't that amazing?" His eyes darted between the two adults before settling back on Ayden. "Do you think you could use some at the farm? I would take care of them when I visited."

Ayden considered the request. His first inclination fell in the mean old uncle category, but then he softened...again.

"You would help with them?"

Rory's eyes shone as a smile covered his face. "Yes, sir. I would help...with whatever they need."

Ayden sat without speaking, part of him wishing for a notion of how to get out of this situation. An idea occurred to him that might change Rory's mind.

"You'll have to clean their pens. They poop. It's stinky, but everything has to be clean or they'll get sick."

Rory swallowed hard but never broke his stare with Ayden. "Poop's stinky. I know. The chickens smell sometimes."

Rory stood frozen as he and Ayden studied each other. Rory seemed determined to have the pigeons become part of the farm's menagerie. They battled out their contest of wills—and Ayden lost to a five-year-old, but he'd find a way to spin it if he needed. He didn't want Dakota to think he was too soft-hearted.

Okay, that isn't the best idea I've ever had. But it's better than nothing, because Rory's a professional at twisting Dakota around his little finger.

"You promise to help me with them?"

Rory studied him for several seconds before nodding. "Yes, Ayden. I promise to help you all the time, as much as I can."

Ayden questioned his sanity and shook his head at the lack of resolve he'd shown. It was too late now to change his mind. He let out the breath he'd been holding in a huge gust.

"Okay. We can get one pair. You pick them out, and I'll let you decide on their names."

Rory danced in place as Ayden helped prepare the birds' cage. Once that was accomplished, it didn't take long for Rory to make his choices. The birds' colors were striking, and Ayden couldn't have made better selections if he had been the one choosing. They finished moving Rory's picks to the transport box and soon were making their way out of the market. With the birds held tight, Rory was ready to leave.

It took longer than he wanted to locate the two women. He and Rory walked forever before he spotted them digging through yet another display of second-hand clothes. Ayden started to vent his frustration but realized he knew a way that would make Kayla squirm and keep him out of trouble.

He leaned down and whispered to Rory. "Show your mom what we bought."

Rory took the cage and trotted to his mother. Ayden couldn't hear what was being said, but the expression on Kayla's face made his smile grow. Rory's hand motions grew larger until he looked like an orchestra leader and the birds added to the symphony. Rory must have reached the 'poop stinks' part of the bargain because both Kayla and Linda wore horrified expressions.

Kayla turned her focus to him and screeched, "Ayden!"

Chapter Four

Dakota reached the conclusion that Jack liked to spend the entire competition trying to be a living pogo stick. As a result, not only were his times keeping him far out of the money, but his butt was being beaten into hamburger. Because of that, Dakota was in a foul mood with zero tolerance for anything, including his increasingly difficult gelding. He clenched his teeth, refusing to give up, even though the competition might not impact his standing. Those days ate at him.

He spotted someone he knew, at least a bit. "Hey, Joe. Could you open that gate for me? My mount's getting edgy. I'm hoping if I let him run for a few minutes, he'll calm down."

Joe nodded and opened the gate just wide enough for them to squeeze through. By the time they worked their way through the crowd, Jack was skittish of everything around them and prancing like a yearling stud. Dakota studied the area and spotted a municipal park that should give Jack room to stretch out and release some steam. With his horse misbehaving, his chance of scoring in the money often enough to qualify for Nationals was almost non-existent.

Jack traveled a zigzag pattern once they'd reached the trimmed grass at the edge of the park. When he got to the lush grazing, Dakota drew to a stop. He had no difficulty getting the message that his mount needed more time to get over his issues.

The horse stood for a few minutes before snorting and shaking his head hard, then eased down to the grass and took a bite. An instant later, he took another step and worked across the verdant lawn. There was no given pattern to his meandering, but Dakota let him wander as he would. He kept a close eye on Jack, and after a while, reined him in and guided him back to the edge of the park, where he stopped to see how the horse would react.

As they made their way through the crowd, Jack behaved as if he were a different animal. There was no contest of wills as they slipped into the pen. Since their draw put them in the middle of the competitors, Dakota knew his run wasn't soon. He planned to use the extra time assessing the other ropers.

He eased Jack to the fence closest to the arena and let himself focus on the other contestants. Over the past few weeks, he hadn't gotten his times low enough to be in the money. It wouldn't be of as much concern if the top prize were spread between several cowboys. That wasn't the case. The winning spot rotated between two ropers.

One of them was a young kid fresh out of high school who Dakota thought was on a temporary hot streak. But he took the other winning competitor seriously. Kit Morris had been a tremendous pain in the ass since Dakota had started competing in calf-roping. They had battled for champion honors for more than a decade. To see him in the lead left Dakota with a knot in his gut. As if Dakota's thoughts called him, Kit materialized as the next roper.

His nemesis trotted across the grounds on his huge chestnut gelding, who was almost as notorious as Kit was. They moved into the box to wait until the factors were perfect. Through the entire process, Kit's horse never stopped moving. The sight of him battling his high-energy mount made Dakota smirk. Once all the surrounding activity ceased, the mount seemed to sense it was time for him to fill his role as the seasoned veteran of the roping arena.

A second or two later, the pair exploded from the box and before Dakota could blink, a rope settled onto the calf's neck. Kit threw himself off the horse, grabbed the now-taut lariat and chased down the calf. Kit was skilled and Dakota felt forced to admire each of his runs. The ride ended when Kit whipped the pigging string around the calf's legs then threw his hands in the air.

Damn! He really is good. Well, I have to be faster.

He waited until Kit's calf stayed tied the required number of seconds then fixed his gaze on the results board. When they announced his time, Dakota frowned. It would take an amazing run to beat Kit's.

As the cowboy rode toward the exit, a smile danced across Dakota's face at what Ayden would pop off at this point with his twisted sense of humor. He could just imagine Ayden leaning in and whispering, *'He's got a tiny dick. You know it's true. Teeny wiener.'*

"You must know something, to be grinning after Kit's last run."

Startled, he glanced over to see Shane standing beside the fence. He relaxed more and gave a wave. "Hey, Shane. How's things? I heard y'all were somewhere in east Texas."

"I needed to check out a new herd bull at a ranch a few hours north of here, so I decided I'd evaluate this competition. I spotted you and decided to see how Jack was doing." Shane studied him for a second before turning back to Dakota with a grin. "He seems eager to go."

Dakota leaned down and patted the horse's neck. "He was ornery earlier, but after a nice walk, he's focused on his job again."

Shane grinned, lifting an eyebrow as he considered first Dakota then the contestants ahead of him in the lineup. Dakota's gut knotted from Shane's scrutiny in a way he hadn't known in a long time, but he forced himself back into focus. As he shook himself from the questioning gaze, he nodded toward his mount.

"He's settling in with a few bad habits, nothing I can't work out of him. Since you were his trainer, I might ask for some help."

Shane's close inspection relaxed. "I'm always happy to help, particularly any fine-tuning that might be easier for me to work into his original training."

Dakota sat immobile for the time it took to run through the contestants ahead of him. When time for his round arrived, Dakota was back on point. Shane tipped his hat then disappeared into the crowd.

Dakota stared at the milling throng as he rode into the arena. He checked that everything was in order before backing Jack into the box. *We're ready. This is what we've been training for all year.* His focus turned to the sounds of the calf racing through the chute, followed by a bang when it slammed into the gate.

He tightened his legs around his mount in preparation for his run. Jack moved a few times in anticipation, pressing hard against the back wall. Satisfied everything was ready, Dakota gave a sharp nod. An instant later the calf took off as if the wolves of hell were in pursuit.

Years of training kicked into play as Jack lurched across the sunbaked grounds. The pair fell into a coordination of muscle and skill that had them darting after their quarry. Dakota had only one goal — catch his calf faster than everyone else. *Everyone.*

They covered the distance faster than a sprinting jackrabbit. He sensed the timing was right and fell into his routine. He shot the lariat out like a striking sidewinder and the rope snagged the calf's neck.

Jack slid to a stop as Dakota vaulted from his back. Grabbing the taut rope, he sprinted to the calf, which had hit the end of the lasso and somersaulted through the air. With perfect timing, Dakota had the first wrap around the legs before the animal hit the ground. An instant later, he flung up his hands, signaling the end of his run. He stepped away from the calf, his stomach in knots as he waited. But his worry was unfounded. The tie held without a problem.

After making it past the initial trial, he waited for his time. He knew Kit's already and thought his score would be competitive. It seemed as if the world had frozen. Dakota's chest tightened and he fought to breathe as the tension played havoc with him.

"And the time for Dakota Neri…is…eight-point-two-oh seconds."

Dakota stood in disbelief in the moment of silence before the announcer continued.

"Congratulations, Dakota. You're in the lead for tie-down roping."

Dakota let out a whoop of joy. The successful round kept him among the leaders in the running. Best of all, he'd beaten Kit. Anything else was gravy.

"The gelding did a good job for you that time. Congrats on a fantastic run."

Startled, Dakota glanced down to discover Shane had reappeared. It thrilled him that Shane had been at the event when everything had gone well. He also agreed with Shane's assessment. "He did great. I think I've got a good chance at the money. Thank God. I hope it's a sign our luck is changing."

Shane nodded in agreement but kept his silence. They watched the next contestant move into place and end with a much slower run than Dakota's. The tension built as one cowboy after another failed to top Dakota's score. With one person left to go, Shane patted him on the leg.

"Looks like you're going to win tonight's roping."

"Damn, it's about time. I wasn't going to make Nationals with the shitty times I've had the past few competitions."

The emcee announced the final contestant and they moved into position. He watched closely, because for some reason the cowboy's ID wasn't given. Something about the roper drew Dakota's curiosity. As they trotted into position, Dakota had the overwhelming concern he might have celebrated too early.

The roper moved into the box and in seconds signaled for the release of the calf. From the first jump of the midnight black horse, Dakota knew another serious contender would be fighting him for a spot at the National Finals. His attention snapped back to the arena in time to see the gelding slide to a stop and the cowboy fly down the rope. The calf was tied and the cowboy's hands thrown into the air before Dakota knew it had ended.

The roper's hat flew off, and Dakota got the surprise of the season when a long, thick braid uncoiled down the roper's back.

"Well, I'll be damned," Shane said.

Dakota kept silent but sweat gathered on his forehead as he waited for her score. The calf stayed tied the required time, eliminating the hope she would lose on a technicality. He swallowed his adolescent thoughts and waited for her official number. After an interminable time, the speakers crackled to life.

"The time for Jordan Capps was eight-point-three-oh, second fastest of the night."

Dakota's heart seemed like it would hammer itself free of his chest as the announcer continued. "That leaves Dakota Neri as tonight's winner. Congratulations, Dakota!"

The next minutes were a blur as he was mobbed by a crowd of well-wishers congratulating him. Once the crowd had thinned, he made his way back to the rig. He ran through the routine of removing Jack's gear and stowing it away. Then he groomed Jack enthusiastically before loading the gelding into the trailer with a feeder filled with alfalfa and a bucket of clear, cool water, into which the horse immediately stuck his muzzle. Dakota watched him to be certain his mount was okay. Once he was sure Jack was in good shape, Dakota climbed into the cab and changed clothes. When he took his phone from the glove box, he saw Ayden had called more than a dozen times. He knew that meant there was a crisis.

He opened the first voice mail, struggling to keep his calm. Ayden's voice started, and Dakota focused more than he ever had for any roping event.

"Dakota, you need to come home...like now. *The Sheriff has been out twice to talk with you. He wants to see you as soon as possible. I'm not sure what you've done this time, but I've never seen him so worked up over anything. Babe, please don't blow this off. I need you to come home and fix whatever happened."*

Dakota's legs weakened and he almost collapsed onto the blacktop parking lot. Dread filled him to overflowing, because he had no idea why the Sheriff would want to see him so urgently. Another handful of minutes passed before he got himself together. He needed to get home as soon as possible.

Chapter Five

Dakota stood in the sterile white hallway staring through the two-way mirror. The faint scent of bleach crawled into his nostrils and left a burning sensation. He'd rushed home once he'd gotten Ayden's message, and it hadn't taken long for him to receive the hideous news. Kayla had lost her life in a multi-car wreck on a foggy morning after she had dropped Rory off at day care. From what the Sheriff had told Dakota, she'd likely never seen the tractor-trailer before it'd broadsided her.

The Department of Children and Families discovered that Kayla had designated Dakota as Rory's guardian. She'd filed the paperwork with the state soon after Rory had been born. He sort of remembered agreeing to let Kayla list him. Rory had only been a few weeks old, and Dakota had considered it nothing more than the overreaction of an anxious new mother. With the tragedy, it would seem that Kayla had everything taken care of and all the loopholes covered.

Dakota questioned why she hadn't given guardianship to her mom, but he wouldn't pursue that conversation. Right now, his focus was on getting Rory out of state custody. The little boy had already spent one night in foster care and he didn't want it to happen twice. The idea of being a guardian might be overwhelming Dakota, but he refused to let Rory down at such a critical time. Kayla's parents were handling her funeral arrangements, which allowed Dakota to direct his energy on Rory's needs.

"Mister Neri?"

The caseworker's voice brought him back to reality. "Yes, sorry. How do I get Rory out of here? He's been traumatized enough."

Dakota wanted to kick himself the instant the words left his mouth. As he'd feared, his ill-considered statement sent a scowl flickering across her face. It worried him even more when it disappeared in a second, and she returned to the professional demeanor she'd used with him all day.

"Rory is enjoying himself, so I think we can go through everything to prevent problems later." She gave him a tight smile. "I'm sure you would agree that we don't want to stress Rory any further."

A whirl of emotions, mostly anger, traveled through Dakota as he glared at the woman standing so stoically in front of him. He clamped down on his feelings and remembered where his concentration had to be.

"Of course I don't want to cause Rory any more pain. The poor kid just lost his mother and spent the night in foster care. My focus is on getting him home and protecting him."

The faint sounds of their breath became the only noise in the area. She shook her head with resignation. "Mr.

Neri, there are dozens of reasons I think you having custody of Rory is a terrible idea. But your ex-wife did a thorough job of making certain you'd be the child's guardian if something were to happen to her."

Dakota bristled, but before he could respond, she went on. "I'll be watching your every move, Mr. Neri. If anything happens to that child, you won't like the consequences." Almost without a breath, she continued. "I think it's time to reunite Rory with his…" She paused, took a deep breath and stopped what she was about to say. She locked eyes with Dakota. "We'll see how things go."

She spun and moved down the hallway until he was forced to increase his speed to keep up. Before Dakota had the chance to think, they were in the room with Rory. His thoughts settled before the youngster wrapped himself around Dakota's legs. Dakota reached down and lifted Rory into his arms. He wrapped his legs and arms around Dakota and held on with a ferocity Dakota had never seen. Rory shook as Dakota held him tight.

"It's okay, buddy. I'm here now. Everything's fine. I got ya," Dakota whispered.

Rory loosened his grip enough to pull away and study Dakota's face. "Where's Mama? Nobody will tell me. They just said she couldn't come get me. Why can't she, Dakota? Did I do something bad?"

Dakota was close to coming unraveled, but he couldn't make himself lie. He wiped away the tears pooling in Rory's eyes before he spoke.

"You didn't do anything wrong, not a thing. Your mama had a wreck and…" he stopped, a knot forming in his throat, but he knew he had no choice but to tell Rory the truth about Kayla. He squeezed Rory tight before continuing. "Baby, the wreck was so bad she didn't live through it."

"Mama's dead?"

Rory seemed on the edge of hysteria, but Dakota continued. "Yes, baby. She didn't survive."

His lip quivered as tears collected until they rolled down his cheeks. "What happens to me? Are they taking me back to the house I stayed at last night?"

"No, Rory. You're going to live with me and Ayden. You'll be part of our family."

Ayden had followed them and was standing by the door looking stricken. Rory spotted him at the same time, held out his arms and let out a soul-rending cry.

"Ayden!"

Dakota fought to keep his emotions under control and realized how much stress had fallen on Rory. He hoped Ayden would be able to help with some of Rory's needs. He knew it would take their combined efforts to give Rory the support he required.

Rory grabbed for Ayden with an eagerness that left Dakota's gut in a knot. He had some idea what Rory had already dealt with in only one short twenty-four-hour period. He was determined to be a father to the boy that he wished he'd had.

Rory lifted his head and sniffled. Dakota resolved to give him whatever time he needed. He heard a sound and realized the caseworker had remained in the room. Dakota glanced toward her, but her face left him with no sign of how well she thought the reunion had progressed. He turned to Rory and found Ayden standing beside him and not looking pleased.

Panic rose to flood his system but when he moved closer, Ayden glared at him.

"He needs to come home. He needs to be in familiar surroundings." His eyes had a glint of steel when their gazes met. "This will be hard on him—worse than either of us can imagine. We're leaving." Ayden turned toward the worker and a chill came over the room. "Anything else you need...you can come to the ranch."

Dakota turned to her and tilted his head. "You heard the man. We're going home."

* * * *

"Dakota!"

He recognized the voice. It was the same person who'd called him at least a dozen times a day since they'd brought Rory back to the ranch, the one he'd hoped to avoid today. He had convinced himself that she wouldn't cause a confrontation at her daughter's funeral. He still kept a slight hope that if he ignored her, she would at least wait until another day.

"Dakota, don't pretend you can't hear me."

Apparently, I was fucking wrong.

He slowed his pace until he came to a stop. With a heaving sigh, he turned to deal with Kayla's mother. "Hello, Linda. What do you need?" The woman before him appeared to be someone with a three-pack-a-day cigarette habit for the past thirty-five-years, a bitter residue from a hard life. Despite the tragedy, he could find no sign of tenderness, only a smoldering rage. He knew without a doubt that, in her eyes, this had become his fault. At least that was the message she telegraphed to him.

She glared at him and glanced around. Dakota realized no one could overhear their conversation, which he knew was for the best.

She got close and hissed. "I've been calling you. I want my grandson."

"It's been busy around the ranch. I would have called when it slowed down."

Like when Rory is graduating from high school.

"And I'm the one Kayla designated as Rory's guardian, not you," Dakota added.

If she could have shot fire from her eyes, he would have been a pile of ash. But he'd expected this face-off. He might be uncertain about how he and Ayden would care for Rory, but he knew he'd never let Linda have custody of the youngster. Even Kayla had recognized her mother would be a poor choice as a caretaker.

She took a step closer and jabbed her finger into Dakota's chest. "I'm taking my grandson home — now. He isn't going to spend a minute longer with you two perverts. Everyone knows about you people and kids."

A rage burned inside Dakota that made a land-eating summer grassfire seem like a backyard cookout. It had been hard enough to tell people he found guys attractive. He refused to let this woman's prejudices affect his life.

"Dakota!"

He sighed and pressed his anger down as he gathered his thoughts. Time stretched out, and the silence grew heavy before he responded to the woman standing before him. She crossed her arms and snorted at him as a sneer formed on her face. With that maneuver, any possibility of cooperation evaporated.

"Forget it. There's no way in hell you're getting custody of Rory. Your own daughter didn't want you to have him. She'd as soon have me raise him. Think about it, Linda. She'd rather have him raised by her bi ex-husband than by you."

Her mouth became little more than a slash across her face and her anger washed over him. To his surprise, she didn't add to her venomous tirade. After a few seconds of silence, he started toward his truck, but she spoke again.

"This isn't over, Neri. I'm taking you to court. No judge around here will accept a Yankee ruling that would give a child to people like you and your sick boyfriend."

Dakota considered her but couldn't keep back his comment. "And just what are we like, Linda? Devoted to each other? Two people who would do anything for that little boy? Why don't you tell me which of your labels works for you?"

"Linda. It's time we go. The family car is leaving."

Dakota glanced over to see Linda's current husband, Erik. He'd always tolerated Erik, although his opinions of the LGBTQ community matched Linda's. Given the situation, relief washed over Dakota that he'd appeared. Dakota hoped he would bring sanity to this moment.

A few seconds later, Linda glanced over her shoulder. "All right, dear. I was just chatting with Dakota. I wanted him to update me about Rory."

He turned to Linda and lifted an eyebrow. "Oh? Well, let's go. You can deal with him later," Erik said.

This time she turned and walked to her husband's side. The tension seeped from Dakota as the pair receded across the cemetery. He stayed in the shelter of a cluster of cedar trees until he thought everyone had left.

He turned to see Kit standing between their trucks. Dakota almost snapped off an inappropriate crack. Kit had done nothing to Dakota, other than beat him at roping every time he'd had a chance. So, he dialed back his response, making it much more civil.

"Hello, Morris. What brings you here?"

Kit shrugged. "I wanted to pay my respects. I've known Kayla since we were kids. My folks still live in the area. Mom told me about the wreck."

They both stood in the growing silence until Kit sighed. "Her mother wasn't pleased."

Dakota tensed at the reference, but he still sensed an obligation to fill in the information this man didn't seem to have. "Kayla gave me custody of her son. Linda isn't happy about it."

Kit cocked an eyebrow. "I didn't know she had a kid. Sorry."

"Rory. He's a real sweetie. I don't understand why she named me as his guardian."

Dakota's information didn't seem to faze Kit at all, but that wasn't surprising. Kit had always been a ferocious competitor and part of that persona meant his emotions were buried deep.

He turned and studied Kayla's grave, and the time stretched out longer than was comfortable before Kit spoke again. "She had so many dreams when we were kids. She wanted to get out of this backwater town, to go to Nashville. Did you know she dreamed of being a singer? I always thought she was good. Now I find out she never made it out of southeastern Oklahoma. It feels like shit that someone never got to chase their dreams." He stopped, never moving. Dakota thought he'd finished, but then Kit turned to him. "We are the lucky ones, though, aren't we, Dakota? You and I spend our time on what most people would think they were fortunate to have as a hobby. We get to play cowboy every weekend, catch a handful of calves and make an ass-load of money, way more than a real cowboy, who spends long days working through the heat or freezing-ass cold without a word of complaint. We're so fucking blessed."

This time he turned, and Kit was clearly at war with his feelings. Like everyone else his age, Kit had been schooled in being a 'real man', in showing no emotions. Whatever he was experiencing, tears were gathering in the corners of his eyes. They stood staring at each other, but neither of them said anything. A minute later Kit turned, walked to his pickup and left.

Dakota studied the spot where Kit had disappeared behind the grove of post oak. He tried to make sense of their encounter, but his phone went off in his pocket. He slipped it out to find a text message from Ayden.

How's it going?

All right. Heading home.

Good. Hurry.

Dakota couldn't help smiling at Ayden's text. It sounded a lot like Rory might win the battle with his new dad. Dakota recognized his little family would have growing pains. He climbed into his Tundra and headed for home. The afternoon was one of those early summer days in Oklahoma when the heat waves rippled over the asphalt. Dakota rolled down his window for the hot, dry air to whip across the bare skin above his dress shirt. His truck roared down the highway with the rust-red soil showing in the drainage ditches on either side.

The drive home didn't take too long, but it was enough to let Dakota gather himself. The old gamecock rooster and a few guineas announced his arrival with more enthusiasm than any modern security system. By the time he'd rolled to a stop a dozen steps from the front porch, Ayden had stepped through the screen door and stood holding Rory.

Dakota opened the pickup, grabbed his suit coat and took the short step to the ground. He paused for an instant to lock down his emotions before meeting Ayden's gaze. Ayden's first words weren't what he expected.

"Sorry about the text messages. I know you have plenty on your plate without my panic."

Dakota let out a sigh of relief and covered the distance between them. He drew Ayden close and gave him a sympathetic kiss before pulling both him and Rory into a tight hug. Ayden trembled in his arms as they stood on the porch. The world seemed to close around them until Dakota heard the sharp snap of the screen door closing. A few seconds later the tender moment evaporated like a water drop on a hot skillet.

Rory squirmed between them until he'd moved himself into Dakota's arms. His eyes showed every evidence of spending too much time filled with tears. Rory pressed his hands on either side of Dakota's face, his stare more befitting someone closer to the end of their life than its beginnings. He waited a moment before speaking.

"You were gone a long time," Rory said. "We were worried you were in a wreck."

"Rory, everything is fine. I'm not going anywhere." He recalled his argument with Linda and the muscles in his jaw clenched. He brought himself back to Rory, held the boy tight and buried his face in his hair. A moment later, Ayden joined them, creating another hug sandwich.

Everyone shook, and Dakota knew they were close to becoming awash in tears again. His own childhood had taught him how to deal with loss. He needed something to take Rory's focus in another direction. Dakota eased back from the tight hug and caught Ayden's gaze. He lifted an eyebrow and hoped that Ayden would be his usual perceptive self. Luckily for Dakota, Ayden seemed to have interpreted his silent request correctly.

Ayden tapped Rory on the shoulder. "Hey, I was going out to check on the birds. I could use your help."

Rory lifted his face off Dakota's shoulder then wiped his eyes. "Ayden needs me to help with the new doves. They don't like him so much since he's so big."

Dakota choked back a laugh and still made an odd noise that had the other two glancing toward him. But of all the descriptions his boyfriend hated most, someone saying he looked too big? Well, Ayden's emotions were easily read.

They found their way across the yard to the finished aviary with its variety of birds. In recent days it had become a focus for Rory. He had helped pick out more residents and it had become a shared interest for him and Ayden.

Without need for discussion, they began their individual chores. Rory had the duty of filling all the feeders. There were several feed mixes, depending on the animal. Dakota had never taken the time to watch them working together. He was impressed that Rory recognized which feed mixes matched with which birds. They said nothing but finished the routines in short order. Rory finished his part of the caretaking before Ayden and fidgeted while waiting for whatever came next. But when Ayden finished, there was no doubt he knew what Rory was waiting for.

"You ready, little man?" Ayden asked.

The two of them moved to a large enclosure at the end of the set of pens. It also had an opening wide enough to allow Rory to walk through. He slipped through and squatted against the side of the pen. He fished in his pocket, brought out a few cubes of bread and held them on his palm. To Dakota's surprise, Rory made a recognizable imitation of a dove cooing.

Dakota glanced toward Ayden and was rewarded with a wide grin that showed off a set of snow-white teeth.

"He wanted to work with the doves and tame them. So, every time we feed, he does this." Ayden motioned toward Rory, who had one dove eating from his hand. It amazed Dakota to see a five-year-old show such control. He caught Ayden's attention and gave him a tender smile.

"It'll all work out for our family," Dakota said.

Chapter Six

Ayden checked over the drinks and snacks he'd put together for the visit with the DHS worker. It couldn't be very complicated. Ayden's cooking centered on fish sticks and frozen fries. He'd been struggling to find super-simple recipes online to see what would work. After several failed attempts, he'd even resorted to calling to get help from his mother. Unfortunately, she had fewer ideas than he did. Her appetizer recipes were from church potluck dinners and they were the limit of her skill.

He and Dakota had no idea what to expect. Tanya from child services had called a few days before and scheduled a visit. It had freaked Dakota out and it seemed like an odd request to Ayden too.

I mean, Dakota has custody, right? Why do a home visit? Rory has been living here for weeks.

But Dakota had reached his maximum capacity for stress, so Ayden had kept what concerns he had to himself and offered to make a few snack things. Undoubtedly it was a waste of time, but it seemed to relieve some of Dakota's tension, so Ayden took care of the details.

His stomach knotted at the sound of Dakota and Rory arguing about what Rory would wear. The fiery sun had already baked Rory to a golden tan, due to his preferred clothing consisting of a pair of shorts and no shoes. There were days when he looked like a refugee from deep in the bowels of the Ozark Mountains. Usually that wouldn't be an issue, since it was the middle of summer on the ranch. But the visit had thrown everyone into a tailspin.

The volume of the argument between the pair increased and Ayden had no problem hearing them. "I don't want to wear that shirt. It looks like girl's stuff," Rory yelled.

"You're covered with dirt and need to change clothes. None of the clothes I put out for you are for girls."

"I don't care. I don't like it. I want to wear my regular clothes."

Ayden saw a strange car pull into the driveway. *Damn it! It must be that caseworker. It figures she would come early.*

"Dakota. Someone's pulled in and it's something a DHS worker would drive."

"Shit!" shot down the hall.

The discussion between the pair ended with the 'I am the dad and you are the kid' part of the performance. The sound of their doorbell filled the house and Ayden checked his appearance before making his way to the entrance. After a last flick over his hair, he opened the door.

He hadn't even managed a cordial greeting before the woman had pursed her lips, knitted her eyebrows and tightened her grip on the folders she carried. Her face twitched as she locked a scowl on him.

"Good morning, Mr. Haskell. May I come in?"

Ayden realized he'd been holding the screen door closed. He popped it open and ushered her inside. He made a sweeping motion toward the living room. "Make yourself comfortable, Ms. Gideon. I'll get the refreshments."

She stepped to the middle of the room and turned while waving a dismissive hand. "No. If you could call Mr. Neri and Rory, that will be all I need."

Without another word, Ayden swung toward the bedrooms. Before he'd taken more than a step or two, an ear-splitting scream filled the house. An instant later Rory shot past, wearing only a ragged pair of jeans. He screamed louder than Ayden thought possible, shooting through the room and out of the screen door before Ayden could react.

A second later Dakota came running from the back of the house, his expression showing frustration at dealing with the five-year-old. Dakota had at least dressed himself before taking on what had become the disaster of clothing Rory.

Ayden cringed at what the DHS worker might have made of the scene.

But when he glanced at the caseworker, she was scribbling furiously in a small notebook. Ayden didn't understand how a bunch of bound sheets of paper could seem ominous, but they gave off just that level of discomfort. Another high-pitched squeal punctuated the morning air.

"No! No, no, no. I don't want to wear that," Rory yelled.

Damn it. How can I help with this mess?

Ayden realized he had to do something. It might be lame, but he had to try to rescue the situation. After taking a deep breath, he blurted out what he hoped would at least change the focus from the growing disaster.

"Would you like to see Rory's room? He had quite a lot of input into the final result."

Tanya turned a gaze on him that would have frozen the local lake. "I am here on the child's behalf. I am not interested in the paint color of his room."

With that, Ayden chuckled. "I think you might find it very interesting."

She stared at him, but Ayden could tell he'd stirred her curiosity. After studying him for a moment she nodded. "There might be something to add to my report."

Ayden felt he'd gotten a reprieve when she motioned for him to lead the way. He knew what they were about to see would be a striking change from the typical bedroom for a five-year-old. Ayden was glad he'd lost the discussion over paint color. The one Dakota and Rory picked would have an impact on this woman, though he wasn't certain what kind of changes it would cause.

They entered the room then stood looking, "I can see there are times of collaboration, but this doesn't do much to change my recommendation regarding your arrangement."

Ayden glanced around the room that was a daydream done in shades of purple. The birth of this space had been a battle of wills too stubborn to compromise. He didn't plan on his viewpoint creating more problems for Dakota. Resigning himself to helping the man he loved, he focused on what he could do about the situation.

Ayden nodded at Tanya. "Let me go check on everyone."

She glanced at her watch before returning her consideration to Ayden. He couldn't keep from noting her expression was more like someone who's been sucking lemons than a person who might be helpful. Still, her next words gave him some hope for a decent outcome.

"Bring them in, please. Hopefully, Mr. Neri can explain."

Ayden shot out of the room before she could change her mind. *There aren't many people on our side. It would be nice if the two heathens hadn't decided now was a good time for Rory to act like a spoiled child and Dakota to show what a stressed parent looks like.*

The two of them were still arguing when Ayden rounded the corner.

"I don't care what you want. I'm your father and you will mind me."

He could see they had moved past any conversation and devolved into bickering, with Dakota only a short jump away from telling Rory the reason was because he'd said so.

"All right, you two, the woman from DHS is digging for one last reason we aren't a good family. Do you want to give her one with all this bickering?"

Ayden was surprised to realize it mattered to him that their little family stay together. He fastened his gaze on Dakota, pulled him close and whispered, "Fix this. It's up to you." With that, he turned and directed Dakota to the other room. His thoughts became darker when he entered and found the woman hadn't moved, but her expression was blacker than a June thunderstorm. He had no hope to save the situation. Ayden dropped into the kitchen and poured glasses of sweet tea when he heard from the adjacent room.

"Mr. Haskell, as I said earlier, I do not need any refreshments."

Damn it.

"Of course, of course. I'd forgotten." He stood at the counter for a few seconds before turning to deal with the situation as best he could. He steeled himself and stepped back into the room. Dakota appeared at the same time, to Ayden's great relief.

"Hello, Ms. Gideon. Sorry we held you up. What can we do to help you?" Dakota asked.

Her face twisted as she glared at Dakota and a ripple of relief went through Ayden. He happily let his boyfriend straighten out the mess he'd created. Ayden had enough issues without adding to Dakota's list of problems. He found the tension thick enough to slice before the DHS worker made a few notes and turned to Dakota with a sneer.

"Nice of you to join us, Mr. Neri. I take it you're ready to speak with me now."

Dakota shifted Rory onto his hip, balanced him then smiled at Tanya. "Sure. We had a disagreement, but it's better now."

With a twitch of her eyebrow, she dismissed the two adults, lowered herself to the sofa and turned to Rory, a charming expression filling her face. She patted a spot beside her and motioned.

"Hi, Rory. My name is Tanya. I thought we'd talk about how everything is going."

Rory stared at Dakota, and Ayden melted at his expression. Dakota gave him a wink and motioned toward the caseworker. After another second passed, Rory cooperated and moved to her side. Once she had Rory settled, she spared a glance at the two men.

"Rory and I will be fine. Take care of whatever you need to be doing." And she motioned them away.

Ayden blinked a few times before taking Dakota by the arm and leading him out of the house, onto the porch and into one of the chairs settled around the screened-in space.

Dakota sat for a few seconds before turning to Ayden and whispering. "Do you think it will be okay? What will Rory tell her?"

Ayden chuckled and settled into a rocker opposite Dakota. "I think everything will be fine. He's been through hell, but I think he's adjusting. What would you have done differently?"

Dakota considered the question, but a few moments later shook his head. "No, I've done my best." He winked at Ayden. "*We've* done our best."

A warmth flowed through Ayden with the acknowledgement of the effort he'd contributed in keeping everything working. He started to comment but realized Dakota was focused on what was happening inside. Ayden relaxed into the chair and rocked.

After what seemed to be hours but was actually only a handful of minutes, Rory and Tanya joined them on the porch. She put away her notebook, and for the first time since she'd arrived, she gave them a genuine smile.

"Why don't you go play, Rory? I need to talk to your dads for a few minutes."

Rory glance toward Dakota, who gave him an almost imperceptible nod. He raced to the play area they had built a short time after Rory had arrived. She turned to them.

"That's a resilient little boy who loves the two of you very much. Somehow, you've managed not to screw up in any major way. He has a few places he'd like for the three of you to go to as a family, like the zoo."

As her words settled around them, Ayden's relief grew. By the time he brought his thoughts back together, they were standing on the porch, waving goodbye to a person who would play a large part in their lives for some time to come. When the content of the last few minutes of their conversation registered with Ayden, he grinned. "Did you catch the outing that your son wrangled during his time with Ms. Gideon?"

Dakota studied him for a few seconds before the entire situation dawned on him.

"Oh. Crap."

"That's right, Daddy. Rory's getting a trip to the zoo. By the time that event ends, we should have a very exhausted and very cranky kid. It'll be a blast."

Dakota scrutinized him for a minute before talking. "I wish I didn't feel like she planned this outing to be a total disaster."

Ayden snorted before walking back into the house.

Chapter Seven

Dakota woke to the sunrise sliding over their king-size bed in the room he and Ayden had remodeled together. They had been dating off and on since Dakota had been in high school and resisted anything with more meaning. However, as they had matured, other partners had become rare.

Now, with Rory there, something lasting sounded more appealing with each passing day. He liked sex. In fact, he liked sex quite a lot. But the appeal of sharing a home had grown, especially with Rory as a permanent part of the family. As Dakota was getting maudlin, Ayden slipped his hand across his chest. The caress sent waves of pleasure over him and he let out a low moan when Ayden rubbed across his erect nipple.

Ayden continued working it, sending Dakota to new levels of desire. It had been a while since they'd been intimate. A small child tended to throw a wrench into the works sometimes, like now.

Dakota placed his hand over Ayden's, stopping the motion then whispered. "Rory will be awake soon. We'd better not get into the hardcore stuff."

Ayden leaned close and planted a soft kiss on his jaw. The hot touch of Ayden's lips caused his shaft to swell with desire as heat swept through his system. Before Dakota could respond, Ayden pressed his lips against Dakota's mouth. The passionate kiss grew as Dakota shared his excitement, running his hands over Ayden's exposed skin. He rolled with Ayden in his arms, pinning him against the mattress.

"Rory'll be up in a few minutes. I'd just as soon not need to explain what his dads are doing naked in bed," Dakota said.

Ayden groaned and strained against him. Their gazes locked, and he kept silent for an instant before winking at Dakota. "I checked on Rory when I went to the john a few minutes ago. He's sound asleep and snoring like a buzz-saw. I think we could set off a tub full of Black Cats and he'd sleep through it. We have time for adult activities."

A flurry of emotions flashed through Dakota, ranging from horror to ecstasy, before he spoke. "If we traumatize that kid, this will forever and ever be your idea." He ran the tips of his fingers down Ayden's shoulder, luxuriating in the smoothness. "I guess we could relax and have some fun. We've been adulting enough since all this shit crashed down on us." He drew his partner close and ran his hand over Ayden's back. Dakota nibbled at Ayden's earlobe before working his way down his well-defined jaw. By the time he reached Ayden's lips, both men were panting. Dakota flicked his tongue across his lover's mouth and he opened it with a moan.

Dakota slipped his tongue inside and explored as they ground their dicks together. The sensations flowed through Dakota, leaving his senses on fire until his cock throbbed. Dakota began teasing Ayden's nipples, which would send his lover to the edge of a screaming orgasm. Ayden hissed with need as he raked his nails down Dakota's back, sliding his hands inside Dakota's underwear and grabbing his ass cheeks. Dakota responded by biting down on the nipple he'd been sucking.

"Holy fuck! That's amazing. Harder," Ayden begged.

Dakota pinned Ayden against the bed and worked his nipples, first one then the other, as Ayden's moans of pleasure grew louder. A handful of minutes passed while Dakota focused on driving Ayden to the edge of orgasm. When he reached the final throes, Dakota jerked away.

A whimper of disappointment leaked from Ayden as he lay panting on their bed. "You stopped. Why?" Ayden whined.

Without a word, Dakota flipped Ayden onto his stomach and pulled his cloth-covered butt into the air. He grabbed Ayden's ass with both hands and gnawed on his muscular cheeks. Ayden groaned at the attention and dropped his head against a pillow.

Dakota slipped the underwear off his man's ass and tossed it to the floor. He wanted to take advantage of their rare opportunity for intimacy and didn't pause before pulling Ayden's butt cheeks apart, pursing his lips and blowing across his pucker. The pink opening flexed under his hot breath and a rolling moan erupted from deep inside Ayden's chest.

"Fuck yeah! Eat my ass," growled Ayden.

Dakota feasted. He wriggled his tongue through the folds of sweet flesh and Ayden sprawled across the bed, giving himself completely. The excitement grew with each passing moment and soon Dakota was ready to move their lovemaking to the next level.

Dakota sat up and gasped for air. He slapped Ayden's ass cheek once, then several more times, until the two mounds of muscle were glowing red. Able to speak again, he leaned close to Ayden's ear.

"Do you like that? Does it make you horny?"

"Hell yes! Fuck me. Give me some cock. It's been too long," Ayden said.

Dakota dove again into the cleft of Ayden's ass and continued feasting. He licked across Ayden's tender flesh, driving the tip of his tongue inside as often as possible. As he fed on Ayden, Dakota's desire grew. After several delicious minutes, he wanted more and could tell from Ayden's moans that he did too.

Dakota snatched the lube from the dresser and slipped back between Ayden's spread legs. After coating his cock, Dakota worked more lube into his ready hole. He shifted forward until the crimson head pressed against Ayden. The tight heat made him almost delirious as he sank inside. Dakota enjoyed the grip around his dick as he ground his bush against Ayden's ass. He froze in place, enjoying the host of sensations. Once he'd calmed enough so he would last over three-point-five seconds, Dakota changed positions again. He inched himself outward until only the crown of his cock remained inside. As a cascade of Ayden's cries erupted into the room, Dakota reversed and sank back into his lover.

Ayden matched the rhythm as Dakota sped to his climax. The slap of skin against skin sent Dakota in a spiral of passion.

Soon he was lost in primal sharing as Dakota pounded Ayden with the intensity of weeks of suppressed sexual desire, and he knew it wouldn't be long before he plunged into his orgasm. Slamming himself with the fervor of a stallion on his mare, he pounded Ayden's ass.

His orgasm seized him with unexpected ferocity, sending him over the edge, and his body locked as the waves of ecstasy washed over Dakota. An instant later he spasmed and emptied himself into Ayden. The sweet pleasure rolled over him again and again until the last wave of satisfaction crested. He sighed and eased himself onto Ayden, kissing down his neck as he returned from his euphoria.

After a moment or two, Dakota whispered, "Damn. That was amazing. My whole body is shaking."

Ayden rolled from beneath him until his lover's stiff cock was wedged between them. He smirked at Dakota and nodded at his hard shaft. "I don't think we're finished."

With a chuckle, Dakota slipped lower until Ayden's cock stood throbbing before him. A crystal-clear trail of precum ran down the side and called to him. He leaned close and ran his tongue from the base of Ayden's cock to the tip, which he took between his lips.

"Yes. Suck me."

Dakota flicked his tongue over the crown of Ayden's stiff cock. The flavor of sweet precum filled his senses as Ayden began to gently thrust. It didn't take long before Ayden bucked into Dakota's mouth and he held on as if he were riding the rankest bronc on the circuit.

After only an instant, the sounds coming from Ayden left Dakota in no doubt that his partner's climax was imminent. Ayden trembled, grabbed his head and let out a low growl.

"Oh, fuck..." Ayden whispered just before he tensed.

Dakota swallowed the first jet. Each time Ayden tightened, another flood of hot cum filled Dakota's mouth as the orgasm rolled through his man. The earthy scent and taste wound their way through Dakota. The final burst flowed through Ayden and he went limp.

Dakota ran his tongue from the base of Ayden's shaft to the loose skin capping off his amazing cock. He pulled off, lay next to him and gave Ayden a kiss.

"That was phenomenal. It's been too long," Dakota said.

Ayden started to reply when a sharp rap at the door froze them both in place. Then they heard Rory's voice.

"Daddy? Papa? I can't get in."

* * * *

Ayden glanced at Rory then turned his focus to Dakota. He'd thought this trip would be a father-son outing, and he could have some time to himself. But to his surprise, Dakota had asked him to help on the zoo trip. He'd been disappointed to lose the quiet time but found he was pleased to be included.

Rory shook him from his daydreaming with a tug on his arm. Dakota had bought their tickets and motioned them to follow him. Once he had Ayden's attention, Rory ran to catch up. The youngster had been bubbling with anticipation at their planned trip and Ayden didn't want to spoil his fun. As mixed as his emotions were about this whole event, he wanted it to be an enjoyable outing.

Ayden spun the kid carrier, one of his contributions to the trip, and followed behind them at a trot. Rory began the tour on pure adrenaline, but he would run out of energy at some point. A rested Rory would make the day better. No afternoon nap created far too much potential for disaster.

A few seconds later Dakota returned Ayden's gaze. A smile grew across his lips and he winked.

"It's been years since I've been to the zoo. I wasn't much older than Rory the last time. This will be a blast. I can't wait," Dakota said.

Ayden chuckled and grinned, "It's been a while since I was here too. I think my folks took my little brother and sister." A wave of sadness washed over Ayden, but he put it aside—not quickly enough, though.

"You okay?" Dakota asked.

"I'm fine. It was just that it was the last family trip before Dad's heart attack. The memory caught me by surprise, but I'm fine now."

As Dakota patted his shoulder, Rory raced back to them. His effervescence brought Ayden back to the excitement of the day.

"This is going to be fun. I've already seen really pretty birds."

Dakota reached over and ruffled Rory's hair. "That sounds great. You lead the way. Ayden and I will keep up. Just stay where we can see you."

The trek that followed left Ayden ready for a lunch break. He found a shaded spot that would work as a place to recharge.

"Hey, guys, let's stop and grab lunch."

Rory wore an expression that told Ayden he would not let anyone cut his trip short. Dakota dropped to the seat on one side of the table with a sigh.

"Sounds good. What do we have?" Dakota asked.

Ayden shot the other two a grin, picked up several containers of food and arranged them across the table. "I thought rice bowls sounded good for lunch." He turned to Rory, "Maybe later we can all get a snow cone too."

Rory considered him before nodding in agreement. "I like snow cones. That would be a lot of fun. Let's see the cheetahs next. They're really fast."

A soft chuckle drifted from Dakota. "We can see any of the animals you'd like. I think later we'll all want something cold."

Rory studied each of them but made no comment before digging into the meal Ayden had prepared. Within seconds, he was eating as he took in the nearby animals. A few times Dakota had to get his attention, but Rory understood they were not going farther into the zoo until he'd finished his meal.

This is harder for Rory than waiting to swim after lunch.

"It's amazing how fast they can eat if it means they have to wait, isn't it?"

Ayden jerked behind them to see who had commented. He found himself surprised at the family in the picnic space next to them. It was two men, one slender and tall while the other measured a few inches shorter and several pounds of muscle heavier. Both were shades of ginger-headed, from a dark red on one to a bright carrot-top on the other.

Like he and Dakota, it seemed they had only one addition to their family. The boy looked close in age to Rory, with a dark tan and loose curls covering his head.

Then he saw one of them aim a glance in their direction. There were so many similarities between the two families that Ayden couldn't resist introducing themselves.

"You're right on that count. Rory is about ready to bust." Ayden held out his hand with a smile. "I'm Ayden and the two troublemakers with me are Dakota and Rory."

Before he could finish introductions, Rory had chimed into the conversation in a voice that would have pierced armor. "I'm Rory, and Dad promised I get to see the cheetahs."

The other youngster cocked his head and considered Rory for a second before adding. "I'm Drew. These are my dads, Mark and Dave. I get to see the boa constrictors. I think snakes and lizards are neat."

The four adults chuckled, but Rory climbed down from his seat and held out his hand. "Nice to meet you, Drew. Snakes and lizards are neat. Would y'all like to go with us?"

Ayden made a quick glance around the group and realized Mark and Dave wore an expression of relief. He rested his hand on Dakota's shoulder then smiled at the other couple before speaking with Rory.

"I think that would be a great plan, Rory. Drew could tell you about his favorites and we could all learn about the new animals." Ayden said.

Dakota cocked his head toward Ayden and lifted an eyebrow before responding. "That's a good idea, Rory. Let's get the lunch leftovers packed up, then you and Drew can lead the way and the old guys will try to keep up?"

The two boys took Dakota at his word and sprinted down one of the wide pathways that threaded through the zoo. Dakota and Dave picked up their pace to keep the two boys in sight. Mark helped finish packing the food back in their cooler. Once everything was in its place, they followed the others at a slower pace.

"Thanks for letting the boys hang out together. I've been nervous about this visit, but Dave was determined to have a trip that would be a good bonding experience." There was a tense pause before he continued, "We adopted Drew last fall. It's been a rough ride at times, but Dave has been busting his ass to make everything as close to normal as possible."

Mark dropped his volume over the next few feet. "I feel bad sometimes, like I don't work as hard as Dave does with the family thing."

"Does he work harder at keeping the family together?" Ayden asked.

Mark jerked like he had touched an electric fence. When the silence continued for an uncomfortable length of time, Ayden considered going with a new topic, but then Mark took over the conversation. "Sometimes. When I can't help remembering what it was like when it was only the two of us." He glanced toward Ayden and dropped his head. "That's terrible of me, isn't it?"

Ayden considered the question with all the weight it deserved. "I think everyone asks that kind of stuff from time to time. It doesn't make you a bad person."

"Do you ever ask yourself that about Rory?"

Ayden didn't hesitate. "It's different for us, since we aren't married and Dakota is Rory's legal guardian. Dakota is so protective of their time together that I feel like a live-in sitter more than anything else." Ayden paused, considering if he should share more of their personal life, including how sometimes he felt Dakota made decisions that would impact his life without discussing it with Ayden. With consideration, he decided he had shared enough with a relative stranger, even if their stories hit a responsive chord. Ayden grinned and motioned toward their disappearing families.

"We should catch up." He gave Mark a sympathetic smile. "We have all the kid's stuff. It won't be long before they'll be looking for us."

With a smile and a nod, they turned to close the distance to their families. Ayden found no surprise that the boys targeted the petting zoo as they wound their way through the trails that made up this portion of the park. The day had the signs of a summer scorcher. Most of the enclosures had a thick canopy of native trees, keeping the temperature bearable. They arrived in time for Rory to tell Drew about the animals in this exhibit.

"Those are horses, but not like the ones Dad and Papa ride. These are miniature horses. And those little ones over there? They're pygmy goats. Papa says we're going to be getting some of those."

Rory continued with the identification litany, while Dakota turned to Ayden and lifted an eyebrow. "We are?"

Ayden waved off the question. "Only for a few days. I'm keeping them for a friend of mine."

Rory demanded their attention. "Hey, Dad, what is that?"

Dakota explained the bird in question was a white peacock, and Ayden turned back to Mark. "We aren't starting our own menagerie. Dakota and I are on the rodeo circuit and own a small ranch outside of Krebs. Over time, we've also acquired animals people from Nichols Hills got and couldn't deal with."

Mark nodded. "That would explain the variety of information from Rory, which is great for me. Otherwise, I'm on Wikipedia through the whole outing to answer Drew's questions."

"No, Rory memorizes stuff around the ranch the same as some other kids learn about dinosaurs."

"Or snakes. Gotta say, I'd rather know too much about goats and miniature horses." Mark dropped his voice so only Ayden could hear him. "We have two snakes in Drew's room. God, I hate those slimy things."

"You know, they aren't—"

Mark motioned for him to stop. "I know they aren't slimy. I still hate them."

A smile quirked at the edges of Ayden's mouth. "Why don't you tell Dave and Drew that snakes creep you out?"

Mark's mouth puckered like he'd bit into a green persimmon. "Well…I'm not sure they'd pick me over the snakes. Dave and Drew have bonded over the nasty things."

Ayden glanced over with a chuckle but kept any comments to himself when he realized Mark wasn't entirely joking. Their silence edged toward awkward when Rory turned to them.

"The snake house is next. Drew wants to see them, and they're close."

Ayden motioned to them. "Go ahead. We'll keep up with the chuck wagons and be ready with any of the supplies our expedition might need."

The next few hours were some of the more enjoyable Ayden could recall in recent memory. By the time they'd reached the trams, everyone was feeling the need for a hearty snack. He glanced around and located a wonderful area. They spotted a table in the deepest shade and he and Mark draped it with a cloth and set out dishes. Soon they had it covered with enough food to compete with a Thanksgiving buffet.

Ayden glanced over the spread and a chuckle escaped him. "I think we have enough for this and still have plenty if we get hungry later."

"We have a variety too," Dakota said.

Ayden hadn't realized it, but for every high-fat and sugar-laden food he'd brought, Mark had something teeming with kale, laced with a zero-sugar substitute and almost devoid of fat. He felt like he was again competing for attention. Dakota settled into a spot, grabbed a piece of cold fried chicken and took a huge bite.

A few seconds later he was surprised when Rory and Drew each took a crunchy chicken thigh and put it on their plates. Macaroni and potato salad followed, creating a mound for each side-dish. At some point, Dave put a piece of chicken on his plate too, but he had at least taken helpings of the food Mark had made.

In a show of solidarity, Ayden filled his plate with generous helpings from Mark's contribution. Once he'd distributed the juice bottles, both families settled into devouring the food.

With a slight feeling of guilt, Ayden had no choice but to admit the food Mark had prepared tasted much better than he'd feared. Everyone took second helpings from all the dishes.

Toward the end of the meal, Ayden noticed Dave kept glancing at the tables on the far side of the area. After it happened a few times, Mark reached across the table and tapped the back of Dave's hand.

"Let it go. We've been down this road before. Nothing you say will change how they feel."

Ayden shot Dakota a quizzical expression, but all he got in response was a shrug. He turned to Mark when it seemed to escalate.

"Something going on that we need to know about?" Ayden asked.

Mark shrugged. "Just the same old stuff. The people seated over there seem offended by the gay couple and their kid. And today they have two couples to work out their issues over."

This time Ayden refused to use any level of subtlety. It was obvious from the first instant that Mark knew what was happening and was struggling with keeping Dave calm.

One couple bathed them and their kids with loathsome glances. After a minute passed, Dave started to stand, but Dakota rested his hand on his shoulder.

"Let me take care of this one. My treat."

He reached down and took a cupcake Ayden had made. He turned to Ayden.

"This one isn't coming back," Dakota said.

"Go for it, big guy."

Dakota turned with the treat nestled in one hand and walked to the couple in question. Ayden watched to be certain nothing looked like it was beginning to spin out of control. He'd seen Dakota defuse situations like this before, so he had faith. A minute or two passed and the scene unraveled. After a few words were exchanged, the couple left. Dakota called after them and held out the cupcake. Without a backward glance, they disappeared at a fast walk and Dakota returned to their table. As usual, he'd played it perfectly, so far as Ayden could see. A few of the other people in the area gave him supportive expressions and one woman shot him a thumbs-up.

Dakota lowered himself back onto the bench. A few seconds passed before Ayden couldn't stand not knowing.

"Okay, dish it up. What did you tell them?"

Dakota ran his finger through the icing, popped it into his mouth and sucked it clean.

At that point, Ayden rolled his eyes and smacked him on the shoulder. "Stop messing with us. What'd you do?"

His expression was irrepressible. "I asked them if they would like dessert to go with the gay floor show."

Mark snorted, "You didn't. You wouldn't."

"Yes, he would. Something about cowboys telling tales," Ayden affirmed.

There was a pause then chuckles drifted from the group. The conversation died away when Rory turned to the adults with a glance at the cupcake sitting in front of them. "You going to eat that, Dad?"

Dakota glanced over at Ayden before turning back to Rory. "I think you should get a fresh one from Papa."

With a laugh, they packed the food and headed out for the other parts of the park.

A while later, they had circled all the way around to the gateway. After exiting, they stopped in the parking area, exchanging awkward pleasantries. Ayden wanted to keep in touch. He'd like to know another family like them.

Dakota surprised him by being the one who brought up the subject. "We should stay in touch. It was nice to share today with another family."

Mark and Dave glanced at each other then back at Dakota. "That would be great, but we're just passing through and thought we'd stop."

"Oh. Sure, if you don't live around here, we can understand a friendship wouldn't work," Ayden said, with disappointment dripping from his voice.

"Yeah, we're going across the country in an RV. We're headed for the Grand Canyon on this trip. It would have been fantastic to share the outing with another family," Mark said. They all stood without speaking until a smile grew across his face. "We're going to move the trailer to one of the shaded spots in the city park and have dinner. The three of you are welcome to join us if you'd like. We might not live here but we can still stay in touch," Mark said.

Ayden glanced toward Dakota and got a nod in reply. With that acknowledgement, he turned to Mark. "Thanks for the invite. That sounds like a lot of fun."

Mark beamed back at them. "Just something light and tasty."

Dave gave Mark a playful bump crowned by a slight smirk. "We bought the bigger RV because none of the others had a large enough kitchen. You won't be leaving soon."

Chapter Eight

Dakota squeezed his knees in an almost unconscious signal and his horse practically sat down on her butt and slid to a stop. Her turn was…adequate. Things had settled down with Rory and he'd been able to work on his roping with a new mount, Rose. She was a new roper Shane thought might work better for him than Jack, who'd never quite gotten to the level Dakota had hoped. Unfortunately, today neither he nor Rose were at the top of their game. The mare became more nervous with each passing second and Dakota shared his mount's feelings.

Instead of focusing on his upcoming event, he scanned the audience for Ayden and Rory. To his surprise, he found the pair in the bleachers, watching his every move. The studied consideration brought him back to this night's goal. He had to get his mind on the competition. He realized several of the ropers had already finished their first round, and he would be up in a few minutes. His center of attention shifted to getting Rose ready to chase down one of the colorful

Corriente calves that were typical fare at ropings in the Southwest.

Dakota found himself drawn back to the scene created by Ayden and Rory. He couldn't keep from smiling at the two of them together as Ayden had an intense conversation with his son. Rose chose that moment to snort and shy away from a passing horse. Dakota realized one of the arena workers was motioning at him to move to the next slot in the roping rotation.

In the normal course of preparing for his run, Dakota would have found a quiet place inside himself to keep from being overwhelmed by everything surrounding him. That wasn't the case this time, and he was anything but calm and ready for competition when the gate opened for him to move into the arena.

All that kept him from a complete breakdown was a double handful of years' experiences in the intense sport of professional rodeo. Calling on that reserve, Dakota moved into the roper's box and positioned himself and the mare. For the first time in ages, he was questioning the choices that had gotten him to this point. He couldn't remember being so disconnected from what was going on around him.

But regardless of what results he wanted, he had to get through the immediate round. In a matter of seconds, Dakota had his mount backed into the roping box. His apprehension had spread to Rose, and she squirmed like a yearling colt during a first session with its trainer. From this point forward, things would probably only deteriorate. With everything situated as best he could, Dakota steeled himself. He glanced to the gateman and gave him a quick nod.

That was the moment the ride went to shit. Nothing in his years of experience prepared him for the clusterfuck of what happened. From the enormous size of the calf he'd drawn to a horrible set of nerves from his horse, everything about this round was bad.

He went through the steps he'd done since junior high and flipped his loop in its first rotation over his head. A few beats of his racing heart later, he released the lariat toward the escaping animal. It settled onto the calf's thick neck and his world moved into slow motion.

The next thing Dakota knew he was struggling with a calf close to his own weight so he could finish this horrid round. After fighting far too long, Dakota flipped the tie string around three of the animal's legs, stepped back and threw his hands up.

The arena became quiet, and he took only an instant to understand why. He saw Rose standing with her head dropped, holding a leg in the air.

"Shit…"

He raced to the injured horse, moved to her damaged front leg and tried to determine the severity of the injury. The first tentative explorations turned out better than he'd feared. But running his hand over hair-covered skin didn't give in-depth results. His mare would get nothing but the best care Dakota could provide.

"Let's get her to the trailer and see what we can do."

Dakota heard a familiar voice and found Shane coming at a fast run. Rose seemed to recognize her trainer and let him take the dangling reins and lead her out of the gate. The guilt of injuring his mount enveloped Dakota as he followed them from the arena.

Shane kept their pace to a slow walk, and it encouraged him that she moved as well as she did. Still, he couldn't help cringing with the pain she showed each time she put weight on the injured leg. He realized a few moments later that Dakota was following, and he motioned the younger man to his side. The cowboy's expression told Shane his horse's condition worried Dakota. That alone placed him in a different light. Shane would have never made the offer he was about to make if the cowboy hadn't shown concern about his horse.

"It looks like the mare will not suffer any long-term damage. So far as I can tell, it's a deep bruise that'll heal," Shane said without turning toward Dakota.

A sigh came from Dakota that left Shane with a smile. He gave the young man a few seconds to sort through his emotions. He waved the cowboy beside him and laid his arm across his muscular shoulders.

"This wasn't your fault. It was just a fucking southwest snowball. You know, where some bad shit happens and from there it rolls downhill, sucking in all the rotten stuff before it smashes into you."

Dakota lifted his hands and shrugged. "Things were going south, but I didn't react quick enough."

Shane ran his hand down the mare's foreleg and got a shiver from her in reward. He glanced back at Dakota and his smile grew. "She'll be fine. Stiff for a couple of weeks, but she'll recover with no problem."

Dakota's face turned into the height of dejection. "Shit! That drops me out of any money."

Shane flashed a smile his direction. "I have an idea, before you give up."

"What?"

"Just wait. I think it'll work."

Dakota fell in beside him with a curiosity that Shane found endearing. He'd thought of a way to help, and as a side effect, it would enhance his ranch's reputation for turning out winning roping horses. A few minutes later, they arrived at Shane's trailer.

He walked Rose to an exercise pen, led her inside and eased off her headgear. Once the last piece of equipment was stored, Shane had no trouble confirming he'd been right and had a solution Dakota needed. He turned back to the cowboy and motioned him to follow.

They stepped around the trailer and found an almost identical pen that held a new female. This animal varied from Rose in several ways. First, the horse was a beautiful sorrel. Besides the coat coloration, this mare displayed a heavy set of muscles, much bulkier than Rose's. He walked to the pipe fence and leaned against it. A few seconds later, the horse moved to the side of the enclosure where they stood and gave Shane a soft whicker.

"She's thicker than Rose, but with the size of the calves they're throwing at you these days, a heavier horse might work better."

Dakota moved to the fencing panel, reached through and scratched her nose. Her response was a gentle nibble. His smile stretched across his face. "She's a sweetheart."

"She's from one of my best mares, but most ropers prefer the more streamlined animals."

He snorted as he stroked the horse's crimson-velvet muzzle. "Streamlined... That's an interesting choice of words. It doesn't matter to me. I'm okay with a little more muscle. She does have to carry me."

Shane reached through the metal fencing and slapped the animal on the shoulder. Her only response was to arch her tail and trot around the small enclosure. He turned to Dakota then motioned to her. "Want to take her for a ride?"

"Sure. Sounds like an outstanding idea," Dakota said. Shane opened the pen and led her into the open arena surrounding them. He'd left the bridle on the mare. Dakota could ride the horse without a saddle. Shane held out the reins.

"Go for it. I can't wait to see what you think of her performance."

Dakota vaulted to the horse's back and a second later he was putting the mare through her paces.

"How's Red doing?"

He barely spared a backward glance for the oh-so-familiar accent. After many years with Dustin, he had no difficulty identifying his husband. The next voice took more to pinpoint. But within a few seconds he recognized who belonged to the second mutter. It was Dakota's boyfriend, Ayden. It threw Shane to see a youngster in Ayden's arms.

"Red's doing fine. Dakota is just putting her through the paces."

"He's as good bareback as he is in a saddle," Ayden said.

Dustin snickered as Shane turned back to see how the riding was progressing. Ayden proved to be correct. Dakota rode with experienced poise. Shane watched for several minutes before turning his gaze to the others. He grinned at the boy and ruffled his hair.

"You here to watch your Uncle Dakota?" he asked. By Ayden's reaction, he'd guessed wrong about the child's relationship. Before Shane could try to rescue himself from the quick flash of embarrassment, the youngster piped up.

"That's Dad on the horse. He's a damn good roper." Rory cringed and looked at Ayden. "Sorry, Papa. I didn't mean to say that word again. But Daddy says it."

Ayden gave him a kind smile but shook his head. "It's probably best to not use all the words your daddy might say. Some of them aren't too good."

Shane couldn't respond fast enough before Ayden explained. "Rory, why don't you go to the fence and watch your dad ride the new horse." He nuzzled the child to where he could observe everything. Once Rory had moved out of earshot, Ayden turned his focus back to Shane and Dustin.

"Rory is Dakota's ex-wife's kid. She was in an accident earlier in the year and didn't survive. In her will, she gave custody of Rory to Dakota." Ayden shrugged and watched his boyfriend ride, but he clearly hadn't finished what was on his mind. Dustin got restless, but Shane motioned for his husband to remain silent.

Ayden watched Dakota work the horse through a few patterns before speaking again. "I like the boy. It's just that everything we do and every single plan we've made has to revolve around him. Sometimes it feels like I'm more the nanny and cook than anything else."

Another long pause hovered over them as easily identifiable emotions drifted across Ayden's face. Then Ayden blurted out, "Sometimes I think Dakota has more feelings for the kid and his horse. Hell, I'm not that old and no one has asked me if I wanted to tie the rest of my life to a roper chasing a dream and the kid given to him. I mean, I was never asked if I was willing to go along with this crazy scheme."

Shane saw it coming this time and made no attempt at stopping Dustin from voicing his opinion. "Shane and I have a kinda similar situation with his...nephew, I guess. He's about the same age as Rory, but Austin doesn't live with us. I think we would love that, but it can't happen. Given the chance, we'd give ourselves to the kid." He turned his focus to Shane. "Am I wrong? I know you agree. You'd take the kid in a heartbeat."

Ayden waved his hand. They dropped into silence to give him a chance to talk. "That's great, and it's obvious you've talked about this...a lot. But everything with us had already been decided without asking my opinion. That's the difference."

Shane took up the lag in the conversation. "Sorry if it seems we're telling you how to deal with your issues. That was never what we intended."

Ayden nodded, although his face again filled with a mix of emotions. "Everyone is just trying to help. Honestly, I'm not sure what needs to happen."

Before they moved into further discussion of their private lives, Rory came running back, with Dakota walking a few paces behind. Shane found himself surprised that Dakota was leading the mare rather than being mounted.

As they moved closer, Shane realized it didn't matter. He focused his attention on the roper and his likely new mount.

"So, what do you think? She moves pretty smooth for a girl as heavily muscled as she is."

Dakota studied the horse for a moment before patting her on the neck. He pulled her close and smiled at Shane. "She's perfect for what I wanted when I found Rose. She's got the combination of grace and brawn that works with my roping style." Then he turned to

Shane. "So is she for sale or did you bring her to torment me?" Dakota asked.

This brought a chuckle from Shane as he rubbed the mare's muzzle. "No, Red's available. She wasn't far enough into her training when you picked Rose."

"I'd love to try her out. If this mare's half as good as I think she is, I won't miss Rose while she's healing."

"Sounds like a plan. We can shift their gear between trailers and I'll get the vet to check Rose. She'll be fine. She just needs some R and R."

"You're ditching Rose?"

Everyone turned to Ayden, who was giving Dakota an expression he would undoubtedly have to deal with later. If he'd gotten that face from Dustin, it would have been an event with more pyrotechnics than Vegas on Independence Day. He waited to see how Dakota dealt with his boyfriend.

"No! Of course not. Even if she isn't the horse I'm riding, she would be breeding stock at the ranch. Most ropers don't need bruisers as mounts." He leaned in and kissed Ayden. "Right off the top of my head, I think she'd work for you."

Ayden's jaw dropped as he shot Dakota an expression of disbelief, but he recovered. "I've always loved Rose. She works with me better than any of our other horses."

Dakota grinned and tipped his hat. "Then it's settled. I'll use Red and you can use Rose and help rehab her when she's recovered."

Rory's voice sounded from beside him. "What about me? Do I get a big horse too?"

Dakota mussed Rory's towheaded hair. "You keep working with Little Bit and we'll see how things are going when you get older. Okay?"

Shane wasn't sure this would go well, but Rory beamed at them. "I like him. He goes fast and never tries to bite me."

With that, they hastened to set everything in motion.

Chapter Nine

Ayden sat at the bar doing the same thing he had for the last three hours — nothing. So far, all he had to show for his time was empty shot glasses and a mug of some craft beer. He'd showed up for this rodeo early this morning, found himself a spot on the fairgrounds and had everything ready for the competition. He'd been eager for this rodeo, one of the first where he'd felt Rose had healed enough to be competitive. But each round still had him worried about a reinjury. In addition, he was going solo this time. Dakota and Rory were attending a parenting class that DHS required.

It relieved him to be on his own for the first time since Rory had arrived. Part of him enjoyed his regained freedom, but he couldn't ignore the nagging impression he was running from his responsibility.

Damn it. Dakota's mess isn't my problem. He is so focused on Rory that I'm left out of everything. Our sex life is gone too. It seems like I don't excite him anymore. It all leaves me feeling like the ugly bastard child.

He shook his head as he lifted the frosty pint to his lips and drained half before setting it on the bar. While still woolgathering about his relationship, someone nearby cleared their throat. He rotated to find Kit standing beside him, sporting a charming smile.

"How's it going, bud?" Kit said.

Ayden shrugged and took another drink of his beer before speaking. "Hey, Kit. How are you doing?"

Kit flashed a dazzling smile at Ayden that left him quivering and the cowboy motioned toward the barstool beside Ayden. "Is this seat taken?" The deep voice with the smooth effect of liquid honey had more than its typical consequences on Ayden. He understood why Kit seldom slept alone. He nodded. "Have a seat. I was washing out a day's worth of dust."

The cowboy slid onto the bar stool and motioned to the bartender. "A couple shots of whisky and a refill of whatever beer my friend is drinking."

A short time later, the drinks arrived and Ayden tipped his glass toward Kit. "Thanks for the refill. Your rounds were pretty solid today. How are things going these days?"

"Not bad, but you ran solid runs too. Nice work. That mare did more for you than she ever did for Dakota," Kit said.

Ayden found himself at a loss for words. Kit had recognized the improvement in his roping skills — and he was enjoying the attention. Part of Ayden's alcohol-numbed brain signaled a potential problem with the turn the conversation had taken. Should this be a situation to avoid? He hadn't been happy with his circumstances with Dakota since Rory had moved in with them and he wasn't sure if their so-called open relationship could withstand him sleeping with someone else, especially Kit. *Do I want to take the chance of trashing the longest liaison I've ever managed?* He could end up single and alone. With Kit, he would just be another notch on the guy's headboard.

"Seems like you have a head start in the liquid courage arena. Should I worry?" Kit asked.

Ayden barked out a laugh and polished off the last of the amber drink from his glass. When he lowered the mug, he studied it for a second before he spoke. "I should be the one who's worried. I'm getting the impression you're fishing with dynamite and I'm a catfish in the pond."

Kit laughed again and gave him a quick evaluation. When their eyes locked, Kit took another sip of his drink before continuing. He leaned in close to Ayden. "You'd be one of the bass. Maybe a trophy-size one."

Ayden lost the conversation for a second before picking it back up again. When he did, the response brought a smile. "Well, so long as I'd be trophy-worthy."

Kit drained his glass and set it down on the bar with a click. "We could go up to my room. I've got a fine bottle of bourbon we could open and see where things go."

He studied Kit for a long minute. *Do I still care about Dakota...and Rory?* He was making a choice here that likely wasn't reversible. Ayden leaned toward doing whatever needed to happen to keep his little family intact until Kit ran his hand over Ayden's thigh and all rational thought fled. "You're getting something started."

Kit finished his drink and set it on the bar. "That was my intent. Do you want to take this up to my room?"

Ayden's head swam from the unending stream of booze he'd consumed. Even knowing he was vulnerable, he let out a shuddering sigh, grabbed Kit's arm and started to the elevator.

* * * *

Ayden sat lightly in Rose's saddle, unsure of how he felt about the whole episode with Kit the previous night. The only thing for certain was that the evening hadn't ended the way he'd envisioned. He sighed as he watched the next contestant move into position.

"Wild night last night?"

He turned to identify the voice's owner and discovered one of the more transient cowboys who only competed occasionally. Ayden wasn't even sure of his name. But Ayden's main concern was the smirk on the guy's face. Given the way the conversation was proceeding, he'd walk this path with care.

"Last night went okay. Nothing to write home about."

The cowboy snickered then shook Ayden's shoulder. "No, you wouldn't want to tell anyone about your little adventure. Kit can make you howl at the moon though, can't he? My husband doesn't need to know about my times with him either."

Several pieces of information dropped into place. First, he remembered the guy's name was Dane. With that bit of reality, he recalled more than enough about him to realize he'd be shortening this conversation by a number of minutes. The dude was a world champion buckle bunny and slept with anyone connected with the rodeo in any way, shape or form.

"Yeah, Dane, I've heard rumors that you can wake the dead during your time with almost anyone. Satisfaction guaranteed?"

The expression on Dane's face was unrepentant. "Hey, I've gotten no complaints. I aim to please, and so long as I get off too, it's all the better." He held out his hand toward Ayden for a fist bump and winked. "I heard you rocked his world and the hotel got complaints from a few rooms away."

Ayden lifted one eyebrow. He glared at Dane until the other man dropped his gaze. A quirk grew in Ayden's lips, but he kept the edge in his reply. "You shouldn't be so eager to spread rumors."

Dane waved his hand at Ayden as if he were part of some elaborate scheme to blackmail him. Ayden found no humor in the situation.

"Look, man… I'm not sure where you're getting your jollies from, but stop. I don't like my personal life being the focus of other people's gossip."

Dane drew back and Ayden sensed him tensing for a retaliation, ignoring Ayden's wishes.

"Well, someone thinks they're better than the rest of us. We both know what you did last night. Kit confirmed it."

Ayden froze. "He said *what*?"

"You heard me. We ran into each other at breakfast." Dane leaned close but didn't lower his voice. "Just to keep things clear, he told me you were a decent bottom but that I made his lights fire."

Ayden clenched his jaws and pursed his lips. He was struggling to keep a damaging personal attack from turning into something much more physical.

One more smart-ass remark and I will punch this shit.

A smirk grew on Dane's face as Ayden tensed his muscles. Then he heard an unwelcome voice.

"Hey, what's going on here? It seems tense."

Kit had appeared in the middle of the mess. Ayden refused to let either of these two damage his private life. He and Dakota had shared buckle bunnies before, but always by mutual agreement. This was a creature of a whole different stripe. He planned to handle the mess before it got worse.

"Dane seems to have dredged up rumors regarding the two of us. I have been explaining to him that my private life is not for public consumption, but he's convinced you were giving him the dish earlier today."

Kit studied him for several long seconds before shifting his gaze. "Dane, my man, Ayden and I need a few minutes. If you could run along and talk with one of the bronc riders, that would be great."

Dane seemed briefly ruffled then shook his head and regained the same idiotic smirk he'd worn all day. "Okay, Kit, I'll see ya later. I can't wait to find out about your exploits after today."

Kit beamed at the other man, drew him into a tight embrace then kissed his cheek. He then spun him around and gave him a shove. "Go find yourself another cowboy in Wranglers. I'll catch up with you next time I'm in town. Ayden and I need to have a chat."

Dane was well out of earshot before Kit turned back to Ayden. His expression was far more predatory than the sweet southern boy persona he presented to the world. But Ayden had seen the other side of Kit emerge before and it wasn't something he wanted to deal with. The whole conversation with Dane had left him knowing he couldn't avoid the prideful calf roper. He readied himself for whatever was coming.

Kit smirked. "Hey, Ayden. Long time no see."

Ayden folded his arms and studied Kit for a few seconds. This wasn't going to end with a mutual agreement. Kit obviously had his claws out. "Dane is under the impression we were more than drinking buddies last night. He seemed pretty convinced that we spent the evening together," Ayden said.

"It seems we remember yesterday differently. I have a clear memory of the whole night, including you storming out early this morning. You might recall what happened through amber glasses. You picked me up at the bar and even bought me a couple of shots and whiskey sours, then came back to my room."

Ayden clenched his teeth and fought to keep his anger under control. "That part you have right. Your recollection of details later in the evening are wrong."

"Well, let me think. Back in my room, I poured each of us a glass of Jim Beam over ice. We visited, and things got hot and heavy. Before I knew it, we were in the bedroom." He shot Ayden a lecherous glance. "It wasn't much longer before you were on the bed on all fours and I worked you like my bitch."

Ayden bristled as his anger flashed to new levels, ready to scorch everything. He squared off with Kit as his fury erupted. "That's a fucking lie. We never got past the petting on the couch. I told you it felt like cheating and you were ticked off. You know as well as I do that I left then and nothing else happened."

Kit leaned close and dropped all pretense. "Look, you little shit. You'll say what I tell you. It's your word against mine — and who would believe your shitface?"

The idea that he was helpless against Kit's character assassination left Ayden dreading the next few days. *How much damage can he do to my life?* Chills cascaded through his body at the possibilities. It didn't take long before he realized the most damaging part of the situation.

"Leave Dakota out of this. He's got enough going on," Ayden said.

Kit's smile appeared more like the fangs of an attacking wolf. "Oh? You consider your boyfriend off limits? You mean finding out his man put out for his biggest rival might affect his scores? What do you think?"

"You asshole. You're the worst."

Kit cupped his hand behind Ayden's neck and pulled them close to each other. His voice, low and threatening, washed over Ayden. "Don't fuck with me, Haskell. You'll lose."

Chapter Ten

Dakota shaded his eyes from the brilliant afternoon sun to see who'd turned into the driveway. The dogs got to their feet and paced but hadn't gone into a frenzy. He couldn't imagine who it might be. Ayden had been acting strange since he'd gotten back from the rodeo he'd competed in while he and Rory had gone to a mandatory class. When a too-familiar white pickup came into view, his world heaved again.

It was his mother, and Judy Neri was a force no one wanted to tackle, certainly not her child. She had quite a few issues with how Dakota led his life, but there had always been a steel-hard support against those outside the family. His mother could be very critical of Dakota, but no one else had better say a harsh word. Her reputation as a mother bear when she defended her own was well-known.

But for the past few years, their relationship had become distant. He lived with Ayden and she'd professed not to have a problem with his boyfriend. Regardless of the reason, they'd drifted apart in recent times and Dakota had never been good at repairing relationships.

Something must have changed for her to travel from South Dakota. He assumed the worst.

"Mom? What are you doing here? What's wrong at home? Is Dad okay?"

Her expression never varied. "Everyone is fine. It's you I'm worried about. I hear you have a surprise for me. I'd have thought you'd exhausted your quota of bombs to drop on your mother."

Dakota stood in silence, unwilling to guess what secret had slipped past his guard and spread among the families in the part of the state where his ancestors had ranched for hundreds of years. Family mythos said one of the early household members had married into the Lakota people and changed their outlook about how the land was cared for and the ranch operated.

He realized he'd drifted into a tangential topic and he refocused. He decided the safest route was to have his mother tell him the reason for her trip.

"What brings you this far south, Mother?"

She looked like a barn cat with a mouse trapped in the middle of the floor, waiting to pounce. He related to the mouse when his mother licked her lips.

"I got a call recently—one I'm sure isn't a surprise to you. Would you like to guess anyway?"

"Linda Morris," Dakota said.

"Bingo! I'm not surprised you got it on the first try. You always had a good mind. Would you like to explain what's going on?"

He made one more attempt at getting his mother to feed him some background information. "Well, why don't you tell me what Linda said and I can fill in the other stuff."

She chuckled and seemed amused. "You've been trying this stunt since you were a toddler. Has it ever worked?"

Dakota shot her a quick grin then shrugged. "It's worked a few times."

"No, it hasn't. I let you get away with it because I didn't want to deal with the drama of calling you on everything."

Dakota breathed a sigh of resignation. "Okay, let me fill you in on all the crap that's been my life for the last few months."

He spent the next hour telling his mother about Rory and how he'd gotten custody. He made every attempt to limit the story to the facts. By the time he'd brought her up to date, she wore an expression he never could remember seeing in regard to him—sympathy. He found himself taken back at his mother's atypical response.

She glanced around them. "Where is he?"

"Who?"

"Your son."

"My..." he found himself taken aback at the unvarnished statement.

"Judy? What brings you to the ranch?"

Dakota cut his eyes toward the new voice to find Ayden standing on the porch holding Rory's hand. A few seconds of quiet passed before Rory took over the situation.

"Papa, let me go. You don't have to hold me," said the child.

Without a comment, Ayden released Rory and watched him move to Judy. Rory stopped just out of reach and studied the woman for several moments.

Then he cocked his head, stepped closer and held out his hand.

"Hi. I'm Rory. Who are you?

She squatted beside the young man, took his hand and shook it. "Nice to meet you, Rory. My name is Judy. I'm Dakota's mom."

Rory studied her for several long seconds then gave her a smile that would melt the ice, even on his mother's heart.

"If you're Daddy's mother then you must be my grandma!"

Dakota almost choked at the words, knowing his mother was very careful to keep the term 'grandmother' and herself as far apart as possible. Rory had a knack for keeping everyone on their toes, though, and that seemed to include his mother. He watched the scene unfold, wondering how she would react.

Shock rolled through Dakota when a smile appeared across his mother's face and she pulled Rory in for a warm hug. A few seconds later, she shook with emotion as the two eased apart. Her smile was loving and maternal, not anything like Dakota had expected.

Who is this woman and what has she done with my mother? She has never given me a look like that.

He cleared his throat, and she turned to Dakota. "Don't be so surprised. I love kids."

"Really? Because I never recall seeing that expression directed at me."

"You were always in trouble...even now. Linda has already given me the breakdown of what a horrible person you are to have destroyed her daughter then stolen her grandson away with lies and half-truths."

He let out a sigh that left no doubt about his opinion of Linda's version of reality. "And what, exactly, did she tell you?"

His mother studied him for a second before continuing. "That lady has seen a world of pain. I wouldn't want to be in her shoes. She wants her grandson."

The words coming from his mother sent chills through Dakota.

This time she won't support me?

Before she went any farther, Dakota lowered himself to talk with Rory. "You go with Papa. I think we have a couple of new cartons of Braum's ice cream, one that might even be your favorite."

Rory's eyebrows shot up and his grin exploded into view. "Black walnut? You got me black walnut ice cream."

"That's right. A whole gallon. Papa will get you a big bowl."

Ayden leaned in and took Rory's hand. "Come on, sport. We'll get you some ice cream."

Dakota watched as his little family disappeared into the house before turning back to his mother.

"All right, Mom. Let's get this straightened out. What nonsense did the nutcase tell you?"

"Don't criticize the poor woman. She isn't coping well. What I want to know is why you are keeping her grandson from her?"

Dakota bristled at the implication. "I did *not* keep Rory from her. Kayla set me as his guardian. It was in the will she did before the accident. Did Linda mention that her own daughter didn't want her to care for her son? She preferred that her gay former husband have Rory. And in case your mind is going in that direction, the DHS caseworker has already visited and didn't see any problems."

She gave Dakota a studied expression as she crossed her arms over her chest. "No problem? Who do you think you're fooling with that line?"

Shane drew his lips into a tight seam. He didn't like to admit his mother knew as much about him as she did. Regardless, it would not do any good to avoid the situation. "Fine. The caseworker said there was nothing she could do to remove him from our house. She wasn't happy about it, but she had no legal reason to place him with someone else."

She considered him and seemed to relax. After a few seconds passed, she gave a decisive nod that Dakota didn't like at all.

"That sounds more like the truth. So, here's what we're doing. Once he's more comfortable with Grandma Judy, I'll take him back to South Dakota with me. A little paperwork from the family lawyer and he'll be a Neri in the eyes of the law. Then Linda won't have anything she can do about the adoption."

She paused for a heartbeat. "You're not the father, right? That would put a kink in our plans."

Dakota stood, his mouth dropping open. His mother had always had brass balls, but this time she'd outdone herself. Part of him wanted to erase her from his life, but he wasn't ready for that step. He was close, though. One thing he was certain about... She wasn't getting Rory. It didn't matter what she bribed or threatened.

"No, Mother."

She cocked her head. "What does *that* mean?"

"It means you're not taking Rory anywhere. You sure as hell aren't taking him back to the family ranch."

At that instant Judy lost any signs of kindness, and understanding vaporized into the scorching Oklahoma afternoon. She became the unyielding taskmaster he'd spent his life trying to please and the past few years working to avoid. He lived his life in a way that pleased him and anyone who didn't agree could fuck off. The family he'd created with Ayden and Rory fulfilled his needs for emotional support.

I refuse to let my mother trap me into a situation I don't want. Those days are long gone. "Mom, you can get as defensive and bossy as you want. You're not taking Rory back to South Dakota." From the scowl on her face, he knew she was about to try to get her way. "Mother, don't. If you pull anything, you might never see any of us again."

The ultimatum seemed more than his mother could stand and apparently was more resistance than she'd ever come close to experiencing from any of her boys. The expression on her face told Dakota this argument was far from over.

"You can't keep my grandson away from me. No judge in this country will…"

Dakota cut her off before she hit her stride. "Don't go where Linda did. She has supervised visitation once a month. I wouldn't push your luck, if I were you."

This time it became obvious she had no intentions of relenting without a major fight. "Don't think this is the end of the discussion. I plan to do what's best for that little boy. My gay son and his on-again, off-again boyfriend aren't enough to keep me away."

"Mother, it's time for you to leave. You have a long trip ahead of you and you're doing it alone."

There was a faint cry from behind Dakota. He turned to find its source and saw Ayden and Rory had reappeared. Both looked stricken enough for Dakota to know they'd overheard the conversation – or at least most of it.

Ayden fled with Rory and a few seconds later, her pickup door closed and a V-8 engine roared to life. He turned in time to see the truck disappear with a cloud of dirt boiling behind it. He knew the war with his mother was far from over.

Chapter Eleven

Dakota sat in the darkest corner of the bar, nursing the bottle of now-warm beer he had been working on for at least the last hour. He'd spent the time reflecting on his performance. It had been another subpar competition for him, not enough to make Finals. Hell, Ayden's cumulative winnings for the season were now better than his. That had never happened before. At this rate, Dakota was considering being the one to stay home and care for the ranch and Rory. Switching off the duties between him and Ayden didn't seem to be helping him compete.

Which brought him to the next thing for him to sulk about. Ayden. Since his last trip on the circuit, Ayden hadn't had his normal chipper demeanor. Well, his typical self at least. Chipper might be an oversell. He thought he couldn't drop any lower when he heard a voice he would have been fine if he'd never experienced again.

"Hey, cowboy. I hate to see your ride ended up rough."

Dakota drained the bottle and used a few seconds to gather his defenses before turning to Kit. "Hey, Kit. No, tonight didn't go as well as I'd hoped. Thanks for pointing out one of my worst competitions in years."

"Sorry, buddy. Just a tough night, I suppose. We all have them." Kit paused for a moment before continuing in his charming drawl. "But I guess I draw in more fun-loving cowboys than you do. I mean, I can't believe you give all the rein you do to Ayden. He's so hot, and with your arrangement, he's open season." He settled his gaze on Dakota and his expression changed to one that would be categorized as a smirk. "Just a little observation from my experience. I thought you might benefit."

Dakota's mood crashed even lower than a few minutes earlier. "What are you saying, Kit? You should be careful about that mouth of yours."

Kit's eyes gave off a sparkle that knotted Dakota's stomach. This was one reason he hated dealing with the cowboy. Dakota's worst nightmare birthed the words that poured from him.

"Better the stuff that comes out of my mouth than what goes into that deep throat of your boyfriend's. He's nice and loose for anyone—"

Dakota attacked about halfway through Kit's verbal jab. He lunged, trying to close his hands around Kit's throat. Dakota missed in his attempt, but his effort shut down Kit's slander. He stood, struggling to get a hold of himself before he unleashed his anger on the slender roper and left him with a collection of wounds and broken bits. It took a few minutes, but he managed to wrestle control back into place. When he had, he shifted his gaze to Kit.

"You're finished spreading rumors about my family."

Kit lifted an eyebrow and glared at Dakota. "If you think you're some tough-as-shit cowboy, you're mistaken. Ayden wasn't that hard to convince to play."

Those words destroyed any control and Dakota barreled toward Kit with an inarticulate cry. Kit hesitated for a fraction of a second before sprinting for the closest exit. Dakota chased after him for several steps until he lagged.

He stood glaring as Kit disappeared into the milling crowd. Dakota considered hunting him down but decided there were more important conversations to have, like one with Ayden.

* * * *

An enormous clash of metal against metal drew Ayden's attention from his work in their garden. It was one chore he could share with Rory. He wasn't expecting any guests at the ranch and it would be several days before Dakota would return. He motioned toward the youngster.

"Hey, Rory. Someone just turned in—"

Before Ayden could tell him to keep working in the garden, Rory took off like a shot for the driveway. *Damn it. I wish he'd listen occasionally.* Ayden was dusting off his hands when Rory screamed out.

"Daddy!"

Ayden froze for an instant before running to the front of the house. *Why is Dakota home so early?* Rory leaped into Dakota's arms and held him tight. Ayden stopped a short distance from them and watched as they bonded. When Dakota considered him, a chill ran through Ayden. Dakota wasn't happy, and he had no clue what it was about. Ayden was already stretched to his limits. He liked Rory. Who could resist that angelic face? But he'd never signed up to be someone's father. He loved these two, but there were days he wanted his life back. Ayden was afraid today might test his resolve.

He studied Dakota as the veins in the other man's neck bulged. It didn't take much to realize that whatever had caused this situation with Dakota, it wasn't going well for him.

A minute passed before Dakota set Rory on the ground and ruffled his hair. "There's a surprise for you in the truck, dude. Take it to your room and give Papa and I a chance to talk about my trip."

Rory studied Dakota's face for a second before shooting off for the truck. A squeal of delight exploded just before the boy sprinted for the house. Dakota stood focused on the sounds coming from Rory. They trailed off and silence filled the surrounding area when Dakota turned back to Ayden.

"Who the hell do you think you are?" Dakota asked.

For a conversation starter, Ayden thought it was an uncomfortable beginning point. He had no intentions of giving in to Dakota's larger-than-life personality. He'd done that before and it had accomplished nothing. He straightened his body and met Dakota's vicious glare.

"The better question might be 'what's crawled up your butt and put you in a rotten mood?' It'd be a bad idea to piss me off. It's not like I'm thrilled to be your live-in nanny, so be careful what you say."

Dakota stared at him for a minute, but Ayden could tell his declaration had done nothing to dampen his temper. His first words confirmed Ayden's fears.

"So, is Kit a good fuck?"

Fury roared through him as he worked to see what direction these accusations were taking. When it appeared Dakota might listen, Ayden gathered his thoughts to form his reply. With a sigh, he began. "I'm not sure where you got this crap from, but I have done nothing in months but take care of your kid. You'd better be careful about accusing me of fucking around with anyone. Where did you get the idea?"

Dakota was heaving his breath like a rampaging bull. Ayden had seen him like this before. It never went well. It gave Dakota a tendency to stick his foot in his mouth and chew on it for a while.

"Kit was at the last rodeo and whipped my ass. As part of his celebration, he found me in a nice quiet bar and told me, in gory detail, how much fun the two of you had the last time you were together. He took a lot of pleasure in giving me the blow-by-blow of the encounter and it sounded damn close to what you're like in bed."

Ayden folded his arms and glared at Dakota. "Why don't you give me those details? I might learn something from your astute observation."

He watched as Dakota paced over the summer-scorched Bermuda-grass lawn. Ayden could hear the faint crunch of the drought-stressed yard. He wondered if Dakota was finished, but he knew that would be almost impossible in the mood his boyfriend had worked himself into. After standing quiet for several more seconds, Dakota started again.

"I'm busting my ass trying to make it to the National Finals. And what are you doing? Cheating on me with my biggest rival. That's a great way to keep me motivated, Haskell."

Enough stupidity had spewed from Dakota, to Ayden's way of thinking, and it was time to set the record straight. "You know, there are two calf ropers in this family. One of them seems to have been forced to give up his career in the hope the other would make it into the National Finals. Does that sound familiar? What do you think, big boy? Want to trade places?"

Dakota's face became a mask of confusion. "I think it's obvious I'm the one who has the best chance at the Finals."

That ignited Ayden like a cedar tree during a summer grassfire. "You egotistical asshole. You think you're the only one who knows how to rope?" Ayden snarled.

"We're both ropers, but I'm the one with the skills to win the National Finals."

Ayden tensed at the words coming from Dakota. He'd wondered if this had always been Dakota's opinion of him. Now the stress of the exchange was forcing cracks to open and showing the weaknesses in their relationship. Worn out and at the end of his tolerance, Ayden knew it was time for him to admit that he couldn't go on any longer. He needed to strike out on his own. He'd envisioned his future, and he couldn't see Dakota and Rory fitting into the overall scheme.

One thing he was sure about, though, was that their discussion was pointless. It drove home the futility of the situation. He studied Dakota for several seconds before turning and disappearing into the house.

Chapter Twelve

Dakota sat in his chair as Ayden carried another box past him and out into the living quarters of the trailer. The number of boxes that had made the trip seemed never-ending. After the blowup earlier, they had kept far apart from each other. Now Dakota watched while Ayden packed almost everything his pickup could hold.

With each passing moment, he considered begging Ayden to stay. Each time he started to move, to tell Ayden how much he loved him, his pride would knot in his stomach and force him to remain silent.

Dakota saved his comments for himself and watched his life leave through the front door. It didn't take much longer before the last few boxes had disappeared. He hoisted himself from his chair and stood in the archway.

"You're really leaving?" Dakota asked in a low voice.

Ayden stopped and let out a long, emotion-laden sigh before turning to face Dakota. "I don't see where I have any choice. You're plowing ahead with your own plans and ignoring everything and everyone else." Emotions rolled across his face as he continued. "You need to decide who you're going to be and what you'll do with Rory. You can't keep jerking him around either. That lady from DHS will come again and she wasn't impressed last time."

"Rory is doing fine, and she isn't coming back soon."

Ayden shifted the box he had been carrying out when Dakota stopped him. He appeared to be willing to have a conversation, which surprised Dakota.

"So, you're working on being off her radar as your main goal. Idiotic plans like that should explain part of the reason I can't stay any longer," Ayden said.

Dakota threw his hands into the air and pushed himself off the door frame he'd been leaning against. The finality of the situation sank in. The idea of losing Ayden sent a chill through him.

"Have you considered everything? What you're doing to our family? You won't be able to see Rory. You have no rights to visitation," Dakota said.

There was a flicker that ran through Ayden's light blue eyes. *Fire and ice. Not a combination I've ever wanted to deal with. Now I do.*

Ayden exploded. "That's it! That's the whole fucking problem — or at least a major part. You don't see me as a permanent part of this family. We've been together for years, but you don't want to get married. Rory came into our lives, and yes, I mean *our* lives, not just yours. None of that makes a difference to you. You even accuse me of sleeping with Kit. And guess what? I didn't." He turned to Dakota with a sadness in his eyes. "Do you have any clue how nice it was to have someone who wanted to listen? It might have all been fairy rings and unicorn farts, but being with Kit felt good. We ended up in his suite. It was a near thing. You don't know how close we were to making your accusations true instead of fodder for two alpha cowboys trying to one-up each other."

Ayden turned, walked outside and let the screen door slam shut behind him. He paused at the top step then turned back to Dakota.

"This is all I have room for. I'll get the rest when I can."

Ayden turned to the windows on the porch and a second later wiggled a few fingers and winked in that direction. Dakota realized Rory must have made his way out of his room and had heard at least part of the conversation. He didn't have the heart to scold the youngster. Dakota wasn't certain what he could say anyway. He'd do what he always did — get them through it.

He focused again when the door of a pickup shut like a crack of thunder, and Dakota stepped onto the porch. Ayden walked to the back of the trailer and opened the door. He knew Ayden's routine so well that he could follow it, even though Ayden was hidden by the trailer's slatted walls. Once Ayden was satisfied, he hopped to the ground and disappeared around the house without a glance at Dakota.

Rory slipped beside him and put his small hand inside Dakota's work-roughened one. He readied himself for what was coming next. Rory had a knack for finding the most painful parts of whatever problem Dakota was trying to deal with. He could only stall so long before he felt the inevitable tug at his hand. With a sigh, he considered the child. "Hey, Rory. How are you?"

The response was to the point. "Is Papa leaving? Are you mad at each other? Was I bad? I didn't mean to upset anyone."

Rory's fear that the problem between him and Ayden was the youngster's fault infuriated Dakota in ways few other things did. He lowered himself to the ground and put his hands on Rory's shoulders. Their gazes met and he understood the depth of the youngster's concern. There was no way he could let a boy who had already lost his mother feel it was his fault another parent had failed him.

Dakota leaned in close, pressed their foreheads together for a moment then stepped back and squeezed his shoulders again. "Papa needs to work things out for himself and with Daddy, and none of this is your fault. Don't worry about anything. Daddy will take care of everything. Okay?"

Rory studied him for quite some time before nodding in agreement. "Okay. If you say so. Then when will Papa be coming home?"

This time Dakota couldn't meet his gaze. He managed to whisper. "Soon. I hope Papa comes back soon, Rory."

At that point, the sound of iron-shod hooves filled the space as Ayden led his roping horse from the stable. The mare tossed her head and whinnied at the sight of Dakota and Rory. Ayden didn't acknowledge the others as he walked her to the loading ramp.

Ayden arranged the space for the horse so it would be as comfortable as possible. When the procedure stretched out for an excruciating length of time, Dakota wondered if the whole performance was Ayden's way of hoping the two of them would go into the house and let him leave without a goodbye.

Well, that won't happen. If I'm going to deal with Rory assuming he's run off one of his parents, I'll be damned if I make it easy for Ayden.

He gave Ayden a few seconds more before deciding to force the issue. "Ayden. Come say goodbye to Rory."

The noise came to a halt.

"He thinks you're leaving because he did something bad."

There was a sound from the trailer that Dakota couldn't identify. A second or two later, Ayden appeared at the trailer's gate. He avoided them until all the latches were double and triple checked. At that point, he made his way toward them.

Dakota could tell Ayden didn't want to deal with the goodbyes, but he didn't care. He braced himself to chastise Ayden, but it was Rory who spoke the first words. He held out his hands, walked to Ayden, wrapped his arms around his leg and drew him tight. The embrace continued longer than Dakota expected, and it had a strong impact on all three of them.

The gloom continued until a loud sniffle came from Rory. Dakota wasn't going to escape a serious case of waterworks. A few more minutes passed before Rory released Ayden and took a step back.

"Daddy says you're taking a trip but will be back. I want to know when. I want to really know too, not some made-up time you tell me because I'm a kid." Rory crossed his arms then stood staring at Ayden.

The fierce determination on Rory's face had Dakota's emotions swinging between tremendous pride and deepest sadness. They studied each other for an intolerable time before Ayden gave Rory an answer.

"I'll come back before it gets cold. We'll go do something fun when I do. How does that sound?"

Rory tensed and glanced at Ayden, and it was obvious Rory had taken him at his word. Dakota hoped that would be the last of it, but Rory hadn't finished with Ayden. He stepped forward again and held out his hand.

"Shake on it," Rory said.

This time there was no hesitation when Ayden gripped Rory's hand. Dakota hoped Ayden understood the significance of the action. Ayden leaned down and gave Rory a kiss on the cheek. He glanced at Dakota, released Rory's hand and walked to climb into his pickup.

Dakota took Rory's hand and the two of them watched Ayden ease out of the driveway. The silence grew around them as Ayden's rig disappeared down the gravel road.

* * * *

Ayden rolled to a stop at the back fence of the fairgrounds. He was ready for the competition — or he hoped he was. He'd never expected to be in a situation like he had gotten into during the previous months. Leaving Rory had been harder than he'd imagined. To top off the issue, he'd promised Rory he'd come back to visit…and he'd set a deadline. Now his daily goal was to get to the next rodeo and rope.

"Hey, handsome. That husband of yours let you out in the big, open world?"

Ayden spun to the voice and found Jordan Capps. Her smiling face was just the tonic he needed for his bruised soul. He luxuriated in the warmth of her personality like it was a warm April afternoon. A moment more passed with him frozen in place when she leaned closer and punched Ayden in the arm.

"What's got a bee in your bonnet? Where's my hug?"

With that, Ayden lost some layers of depression he'd taken on when he'd left the ranch. He lunged forward, wrapped his arms around Jordan and gave her a fierce hug. An instant later she slipped her arms around him, returning his embrace with equal ferocity. The two of them swayed back and forth then she released him, grabbing his shoulders and holding him at arm's length. She studied him the same way he would a new herd sire. As it began to feel awkward, she stepped back and shifted her hands to her hips.

"You and lover boy are having issues, aren't you? And I had such high hopes. Well, tell me what happened. Auntie Jordan can help you salvage the relationship."

Ayden leaned against the truck and let out a sigh that should have rattled the dried remnants of his relationship with Dakota. He shook his head but knew he would tell Jordan the story.

"Dakota came home from a rodeo and was yelling at me about sleeping with Kit. Just all kinds of stupid bullshit."

"Did you?"

"Did I *what*?"

Jordan sighed and rolled her eyes. "Don't pull the dumb country boy routine with me. I've been listening to your junk since we were doing peewee rodeos. Kit's everyone's type. So the question is…did you?"

Ayden puffed up like a bantam rooster. Then he saw Jordan's cocked eyebrow and wilted. "Not exactly…"

Jordan sighed again. "Sounds a lot like trying to say a blowjob isn't sex."

Ayden snorted and continued. "It wasn't like that. Yes, we ended up in his room and he was putting his patented moves on me."

"And you had a dose of morality?"

"Oh, shut up." He paused for a second. "Yeah, I guess you weren't that far from the truth. The important part is nothing happened."

"You were in Kit Morris' room and nothing happened?"

"Hard to believe, isn't it? Still, it's the truth."

"I'm guessing Dakota didn't trust you?"

Ayden considered the question for quite some time. Then he shook his head as he explained. "It wasn't him. It was me. I've had it. I deserve a life too, and no one has asked me what I wanted since Dakota's life unraveled when Kayla died."

Jordan studied him for a second before motioning him to the RV she used. He followed her like a new puppy. Without a word, she motioned him to a recliner while she fussed at the pantry and gathered a variety of food.

"Jordan, you don't need to—"

She held out her hand to silence him. "This doesn't even count. The sandwich makings were from last night and the hot chocolate won't take but a minute. The only way I'll get the details from you is if you're sugared up and stuffed with food."

That was the end of the conversation. Ayden had lost.

While he waited, he spent the time checking out the living quarters in Jordan's trailer. The only word that worked was 'quaint'. He knew if he called it that in front of Jordan, she might hit him with a skillet. It was cute as hell. Jordan had created most of the interior pieces herself. As if she could read his mind, she said,

"My little brother helped with the construction. He's the builder in the family."

He scanned the room again, enjoying the décor, then Jordan called him from his diversionary tactic.

"We can talk about my mad skills at interior decorating later. What happened between you and your man? I mean, he accused you of cheating with Kit and you left his ass." She lifted her hands in a shrug. "That don't make no sense, buddy."

Ayden watched as she cut the sandwich in half, passed one to him and took a bite out of the other. She watched him pick at his sandwich until Ayden set it on the table and met her gaze.

"I'm tired of being the nanny slash housekeeper. I know I sound like a little bitch, but no one asked if I wanted to be a parent. He's a good kid, but it wasn't anything I ever wanted with any kind of deep, burning desire."

Jordan wiped her mouth without adding any comment. She took another bite of the enormous sandwich and motioned for him to continue.

"What else do you want to know? It wasn't a horrible knock-down, drag-out fight, but I have to go on with my life while Dakota struggles to keep a kid that isn't even his." He wagged his finger at Jordan as his story progressed. "Just to make things more interesting, he has Linda Morris dragging him through court to get custody of Rory. And to make it even more amusing, his mom is fighting to get Rory too."

Jordan let out a low whistle. "Judy Neri is not someone normal people fight with. It's too easy to lose that argument."

Ayden snorted and took a bite of the sandwich he'd picked up from the table. Once he could talk again, he pointed the sandwich at Jordan. "It sure looked like her son could meet her barb for barb. Dakota told her to leave and that Rory wouldn't be with her. It was impressive."

"Wow! I'll be waiting for the sun to rise in the west tomorrow. I didn't know when—or even if—your man would ever defy his mother. The kid must be important to him for him to buck the matriarch of the Neri clan."

Ayden shook his head and considered her comment. He explained, "Rory was a part of Dakota's life before me. He was a tiny baby, though, and Dakota didn't see him often. It was obvious he loved the kid. He never turned Kayla down when she asked him to babysit." Ayden shook his head. "Maybe that's it. Maybe I wanted to get Dakota's attention at the same level he gave it to Rory."

"It's tough to compete with someone's kid. You must know that."

Ayden's emotions bubbled over as Jordan hit one of his sensitive points. "That's just it. Rory *isn't* Dakota's kid. Kayla had a thing with some guy right after she divorced him. She said it was a fling, and the guy disappeared as soon as she told him he was the daddy."

Jordan seemed concerned as she studied him. After a short time had passed, he sighed and said, "Yes, I wondered about it being convenient timing, but Kayla never varied from her story. Her mother even said she's met Rory's daddy once."

Jordan held his gaze for a minute longer before shrugging. "I guess it doesn't matter anymore. Kayla is gone, and if there was a secret, it went with her."

"Yeah, I guess that's right. She was only part of the issue. I'm sure everyone will decide I'm the asshole this time," Ayden said.

"It takes two to screw things up. Back to the issue at hand… You left Dakota and are back on the circuit. From what you said, you are done with Dakota and his son. That sounds pretty final." She paused again and seemed to consider Ayden before continuing. "Besides, didn't you two have an open relationship?"

"Exactly! I mean, I didn't do anything with Kit. Still, we had talked it to death and decided we wanted flexibility. To make it even worse, Dakota was the one who wanted to keep the relationship open." Ayden cringed at the hysterical note in his voice.

"Just out of curiosity, how often did this sharing happen?" Jordan asked.

"A few times. Just some damn buckle bunnies."

Jordan snorted at the moniker. "Buckle bunnies? What the hell is that?"

This time Ayden relaxed enough to chuckle at his own comment. "Buckle bunnies are what Dakota calls the twinks who want to do cowboys. You know…trophy buckles and they're trying to get laid, like a notch on the bedpost and that kind of junk. He heard it somewhere and got me using it. It worked at least one way. The name makes me laugh."

Jordan held her hand over her mouth as she clearly struggled not to burst out in giggles. Within a few seconds, she got herself under control. "Okay, I'll give him that one. Back to my question… It doesn't seem to be an open relationship. It sounds more like a polyamorous relationship. From your reaction, you weren't happy with the idea and Dakota didn't think it was too cool for you to be with someone else. Sounds like neither of you wanted what you claimed you did."

Ayden rolled his eyes and held up his hands. "Okay, fine. I still don't have a life if I do nothing but take care of Dakota. Even worse, he gets to be the perfect dad while I'm like a hired guy. It's my turn, and I plan to enjoy it."

Waves of sadness showed across Jordan's face as Ayden watched. Then she dropped her chin to her chest. "I hope you find what you're looking for, Ayden. You might wind up with nothing. Seems you need to talk it out with Dakota…but what do I know?"

Jordan was one of the most perceptive people he knew. Her opinion counted for quite a lot with him. But this time he questioned her insight. He'd spent months taking care of everything at the ranch and he was tired of the whole thing. He was only twenty-five, and his relationship with Dakota wasn't going anywhere. Well…nowhere that he found interesting.

"Yo! Ayden, Ayden, you still with me?"

He gave her a sheepish grin. "Was I gone for a minute? Sorry about that." With a wink, Ayden changed the conversation. "Are you roping tonight? It's been a while since I've competed. A few pointers would be very helpful."

"Get yourself ready, cowboy. You're fixin' to get the biggest ass whooping of your life." Her grin turned something close to evil. "And a girl will do it."

A huge smile spread across Ayden's face as he turned and raced for his horse.

Chapter Thirteen

Dakota sat and watched Rory work intently at the trailer's table. As the boy mashed the clay, a grin was stretched across his face. Parts of their lives together were going fine and others not. So far, Rory followed Dakota's instructions when he stayed at the trailer with whatever adult Dakota could find to watch the boy while he competed.

"Look, Daddy. I made you a burger."

Startled, Dakota focused on what Rory had spread over the table. It was a sandwich in primary colors. Bits of Play-Doh covered the desk while the big chunks sat in containers under the window. Dakota moved closer so he could study what Rory had created.

He scrutinized the five-year-old's work. Purple buns and orange pickles...*an interesting choice.* He pointed to a flat green pancake-shaped object in the middle. "What's this part?"

"Daddy, you're so funny. That's the lettuce. Papa says it's the most important ingredient."

A knot formed in his stomach at the mention of Ayden. Rory'd had a lot of trouble adjusting when Ayden had first left. He didn't want to stir up all those bad feelings again. He waited a few seconds before reaching over and ruffling Rory's cotton-top hair. "It's really original. Why don't you tell me about it?"

Rory filled the next few minutes with the most creative description of his sculpture Dakota had heard in his life. From dragon-fire pickles to lettuce crunch, it was a wild story of his imaginary cooking adventures. They had covered all the possibilities when Rory turned to him. He could see the tears forming in the youngster's eyes. He shriveled inside, knowing what the eventual ending would be.

"Do you think Papa would like it? I could make him one too, just like he used to make me from the TV shows. I could make it really good."

He wrapped Rory in his arms and held him tight. Seconds later, Rory hugged him back. They stayed like that until Rory pulled away. He rested his arms on Rory's shoulders and leaned in to give him a light kiss. "He would love it if you made him a burger too. You make it and I'll figure out some way to get it to your papa."

Rory studied Dakota until he found some kind of validation. The gloom lifted after a few minutes and Rory was once again deep in his project. Once things had settled, Dakota wondered how he would fulfill his promise to get the creation to Ayden. He had a couple of ideas. He glanced at his watch and realized the hand-off needed to happen in the next few hours.

"Rory, Daddy needs to check with some people to find Papa. You stay inside and work on that burger. Okay?"

"Okay. I'll stay right here." He grinned at Dakota. "I'll make you another one too."

"I'd like that a lot. I'll be back in a minute. Don't answer the door either. Daddy has a key, so you won't need to worry about who it might be."

Rory bobbed his head like a bird at a winter feeder. "I'll be careful."

Dakota gathered his stuff, glanced at Rory then stepped out of the door. He listened and heard nothing. At that point, he headed out to see if he could find the one person who might know which roping event Ayden was competing in this weekend.

He'd made his way down several rows of travel trailers belonging to the competitors before spotting the person he'd been searching for. He yelled out at the briskly moving figure.

"Hey! Jordan."

She slowed to a stop and turned to Dakota. Her expression seemed to be a combination of warring emotions. He focused on Jordan as he moved to intercept her, but somehow, she avoided making eye contact. After trying to get her attention — and failing — he broke into a run. When he was close enough that she couldn't say she hadn't understood him, he called out again.

"Jordan. Hey, Jordan, hang on. I need to talk with you."

She stopped this time, even if her primary emotion seemed to be resignation. When Dakota had closed the distance to only a few steps, Jordan turned to him and crossed her arms. Her expression warned him to watch what he said. He considered for an instant before deciding to plunge forward.

"Rory is missing Ayden. I hoped you might know where he'd be at."

"Are you fucking kidding me? After the crap you pulled?" Jordan asked.

Dakota took a step back in response to the fire in Jordan's eyes. There was no doubt he had made the top of her shit list. He stepped back to give them breathing space. After a few seconds of silence, Jordan began.

"Don't act like you don't know why he's hurt. You made him feel like he had no input into the life y'all were creating. Hell, you know if you'd asked, he would have married you in a New York second. Then you'd be legal—and married. Did you ever consider that? Then he would have rights to the kid and the game you're playing would be different. Where would that leave you? Well? What do you think, big boy?"

He'd reached a new level of confusion and his fear of Jordan increased. He wasn't certain how this would go down. He still felt responsible for what he'd caused.

"Okay. I understand you're upset with me. I want to point out that Ayden left Rory and me, not the other way around."

"And the whole thing with accusing him of sleeping with Kit? Was that just for shits and giggles?"

Dakota's heart sank at the righteous indignation coming from Jordan. Her anger directed at him seemed unfair. "Kit was the one who told me Ayden had cheated. Then Ayden left. I don't know. Maybe we could have talked it out, but I never got that option, so don't get all self-righteous about your buddy Ayden."

A sound of pure disgust came from Jordan as she leaned in close. Dakota wondered about the source of her fury but knew this wasn't the time. He wouldn't leave the discussion and not defend himself.

Jordan pursed her lips and stared at him until he wondered when she would speak. Regardless, he knew the conversation hadn't ended. "Have you talked to Ayden? Did it ever occur to you that he might want to have input into your lives together?"

This time the emotions that ruled Dakota were confusion and frustration. He struggled to recall their discussions, time after time, about how they would work Rory into the day-to-day bits of their lives. Since Ayden spent more time with the youngster, Dakota tried to have him lead the conversations about how they would deal with the daily tasks of Rory's care. He turned to Jordan, feeling falsely accused.

"Ayden made all those decisions. Well, we made them together. He was the one to care for Rory though, not me. Since he was my kid, I kinda assumed I had to make the final decision. I didn't want anyone to blame Ayden if the shit hit the fan."

Jordan considered him for several long seconds before she continued. Dakota thought she might have softened her opinion. He discovered the shift was minor.

"You should have worried less about how everything made *you* feel and more about how it would make Ayden feel. Don't you ever consider how your actions might affect someone else? Dakota Neri, you are one of the most self-centered people I've ever met in my life."

As Dakota focused on the torrent of words spewing out of Jordan, he realized the surrounding sounds. The drifts of words coming from the people around them caught his awareness. The crowd was trying to find something, but none of it was directed at the public display he and Jordan had created. Then he overheard words that changed his blood to ice. Fire was racing through the campground.

His only thought was of Rory alone in the trailer, and he'd been so proud of the prime spot under the shade of the blackjack oaks. Now all he could see in his mind's eye was a thirty-foot tall barrier of flame racing through the trees. He left at a dead run, hoping he wasn't too late. He detected the odor of fire and his gaze fastened on the smoke billowing ahead of him. Dakota prepared himself to find a disaster when he raced around the corner to the last place he'd left his son. He prayed the whole trailer wasn't in flames.

He almost fell to his knees in relief when he got to the RV and found the fire had gone in the opposite direction. He realized people were packing the campground, trying to see what had happened and if anyone needed help.

Dakota scanned the area for Rory. His fear grew to overwhelming levels as he sprinted through the tendrils of smoke. He ran to the trailer and pounded on the door.

"Rory! Are you in there? Open the door for Daddy."

He waited a few seconds, his heart crashing when there was no answer. He fumbled for his keys and unlocked the door. Far too long passed before he finessed the key into the lock.

The second he opened the door, it exploded outward, and a terrified child clung to him with a determination that left no doubt in Dakota's mind that taking Rory on the circuit had been a mistake.

"I didn't leave, Daddy. It was scary, but I did what you told me. I stayed in the trailer, no matter what. I'm glad you came back."

Dakota could sense the notes of panic in Rory's voice and the quiver that told him Rory was close to tears. He held the child tight against him and struggled to keep his own emotions under control. They held each other as the crowds swirled past them.

Once Dakota was certain all their belongings were intact, he grabbed Rory and went to see how the firefighting efforts were going. He jumped at the sound of a juniper bursting into flames.

"Daddy, this is scary," Rory said.

"It is. Let's go inside and I'll fix you a peanut butter and jelly sandwich with toasted bread and everything, just like you like it."

"That sounds good. I like PB and J sandwiches," Rory said.

Dakota held Rory's hand while he fumbled to open the door. It would have been easier to let go of Rory's hand, but at this point, he refused to let the youngster out of his grasp. He had struggled with the latch far too long when someone close cleared their throat. He snapped his head up to find Jordan standing a few steps away. After a long silence, Dakota decided to see what she would add to the mess he'd made. He chastised himself anew every time he reflected about what things could have gone wrong with Rory, alone in the trailer. He was only a hair's breadth from losing his shit over that decision.

To his surprise, Jordan held out her hands and motioned toward the boy. "Give him to me before you drop him." When Dakota hesitated, she rolled her eyes, stepped close and plucked him from Dakota's arms. Rory leaned back and his expression almost pulled laughter from a day that was far too close to tragic.

Jordan motioned to the trailer door. Her tone this time was much closer to a low growl. "Get the door open. You don't want what I'm about to tell you to be said where anyone else can hear me."

Dakota started to object but he was certain Jordan wasn't bluffing. He focused on the door latch, and within a few seconds, they were standing in Dakota's living space. Jordan lowered Rory to the floor and nudged him toward his play area. She watched with a critical eye until Rory was distracted. She clearly wanted to keep the drama from Rory. Dakota winced when she turned to him. Her expression illustrated her disdain. She motioned him to the dining table and slid in opposite him. She leaned close and her words were almost a hiss.

"You left him in the trailer? What is he…five? You walked off and left a kid alone while you ran around. Are you a complete idiot? I hope the fire gave you a sampling of what could happen. Did it make you want to puke when you thought of Rory trapped in your travel trailer, way too close to a huge-ass fire?"

This time Jordan's description had its desired effect on Dakota. After a few seconds of creating the scene in his imagination, he became light-headed and nauseous. His opinion of himself began to match hers. He realized the extent of his impact when Rory stopped what he was doing, walked across the room and took his hand.

"You okay, Daddy?"

Dakota looked into the earnest face before him and couldn't keep from leaking a few tears. He cupped Rory's face in his hands and gave him a tender kiss. "Everything's okay. Aunt Jordan just explained to Daddy what a bad idea it was for you to stay in the trailer by yourself. We won't ever do that again."

Rory considered him before nodding his agreement. "That is a good idea, Daddy. It was scary when it smelled smoky and people were running around. But I was a good boy and did what you said and didn't leave."

Dakota squashed down the nausea at Rory's description. When he turned to Jordan, her expression surprised him. Rather than the varied levels of rage he had seen during the day, there was a look of curiosity.

"What?" Dakota said.

"I'm Aunt Jordan?"

Dakota chuckled. "You sound like an older sister who is snapping her brother into behaving like he should."

The description seemed to leave Jordan at a loss for words. When she spoke, it wasn't what he expected. "I can watch Rory during your run tonight." Her expression regained some of its former sour demeanor. "But don't expect me to bail you out any more. You need to talk to Ayden."

Rory perked up at the mention of Ayden. He tugged on Jordan's sleeve until she acknowledged him. "Hey, bud. What's up?"

"Do you know my papa? He's a roper, but he said he would visit. I haven't seen him." Rory seemed close to bursting into tears. "Have you? I miss him a whole bunch."

This time Rory's words must have struck close to Jordan's heart. She flicked her sleeve across her eyes and smiled, the first one Dakota had seen from her today.

"Your papa is in Little Rock at a roping. I'll see him in a day or two and I'll remind him he promised to come see you."

With that taken care of, she returned her focus to Dakota. "He may have jumped the gun on some decisions he's made, but that doesn't mean he's wrong. It's worth taking another look at…whatever the two of you had." She glanced at Rory before continuing. "Mostly y'all owe a certain kid a stable place to grow up. He's already been through more than anyone his age deserves."

Dakota started to defend his decisions, but one glance at the expression on Jordan's face told him to keep his mouth shut and count himself lucky the day hadn't turned out more tragic. After a moment's hesitation, he turned to Jordan.

"How about one of our special peanut butter and jelly sandwiches?"

She lifted one eyebrow with agonizing slowness and studied him. Then her expression changed to a warm smile and she replied, "Sounds yummy."

Chapter Fourteen

Dakota filled the water tubs from the five-gallon buckets he carried. He smiled at the slurping sound the horses made as they drank the fresh water. After a quick refill, he moved to the calves' pen, and they sprinted to intercept him. He couldn't keep from chuckling at how disappointed they would be once they discovered he'd only brought water and not the molasses-coated grains they got in the evening. Once they realized it wasn't the treats, the handful of calves grazed their way back into their pasture. Dakota spent a few minutes riding among them each day to gauge their health.

Today's peace shattered when Rory tore out of the house yelling at the top of his voice. "That lady's coming. She's coming, Daddy." Dakota struggled to make heads or tails of what the boy was talking about. 'That lady' could be any one of a dozen women whose lives intersected with his. He couldn't imagine any of them getting that kind of response from Rory. *Well,*

*there's only one way to figure it out and that involves me
moving my butt out front to see who has arrived.*

Dakota stacked the buckets in the feed room,
accompanied the entire time by a very anxious Rory,
who was making more noise than both dogs combined.
More confused than anything else, Dakota dusted his
hands off as he rounded the corner of their white ranch
house. He wiped off the final bits of grime as the car
rolled to a stop.

A knot formed in his throat at the sight of the dark
SUV in front of the house. He had just gotten his shit
together, and he'd hoped to have more time before he
dealt with their case worker. Their contact had never
been that cordial, but he'd always set up everything so
she couldn't do more than scowl at him as she left the
ranch at the end of each visit. Those evaluations had all
been planned, and he'd been prepared.

This arrival was a surprise. He glanced at Rory and
the child grimaced. When their eyes met, Rory
whispered to him, "See? It's the lady. It's always bad
when she's here."

Dakota kept any comments to himself, but on the
inside he agreed with Rory. Nothing good happened
when Tanya Gideon arrived. Her goal from their first
meeting seemed to be to put Rory in a different home.
She'd been at their house at least a dozen times since
then. It hadn't taken Rory long to categorize the worker
as one of those people who brought tension and strife
into their lives. Dakota chastised himself for not
knowing Tanya was Rory's 'lady'.

She sat in her car, leaving the engine running,
probably to mitigate the heat of the day. While waiting
for her to gather whatever paperwork she needed, he
and Rory stood in the shade of the cluster of chinaberry

trees that grew in the yard's corner. Rory eased beside him and Dakota patted Rory's white-blond hair. A few more seconds passed and Rory locked gazes with Dakota.

"What's she doing?" Rory asked. "She could talk to us so we can answer her questions."

The logic of his response took Dakota by surprise, but it shouldn't have. Rory was a bright kid and his insights continued to bring that point to Dakota's attention. Before he could respond to the little boy's question, the dark car door opened and the harried-looking woman climbed out and marched toward them. She looked as grim as ever as she approached the pair. One glance and Dakota knew their conversation wouldn't be pleasant. Since this was an unscheduled meeting, Dakota thought it would be in his own best interest to let her drive the discussion. As he'd predicted, she didn't wait long before starting.

"Mr. Neri, I'm here to discuss several complaints that have been registered regarding your custody of Rory."

Dakota bristled at the implication he was not taking care of Rory like he should. She'd never been so blunt before. The change in tactic sent a ripple of dread through him. He tried to keep everything calm as he reviewed his options. The only objection that might have any basis had to have originated from Kayla's mother — Linda Morris.

"I haven't seen Mrs. Morris in several weeks, if not longer. I don't know what trouble she'd have about how I'm taking care of Rory. Well, none that were new."

Tanya dabbed her kerchief across her face as she shook her head. "It isn't from Mrs. Morris. A complaint was filed stating you left this child by himself and unsupervised." Her expression was of extreme self-vindication. There was no doubt she felt that her predictions had been correct.

Dakota studied her for a long minute, but he knew time was limited. He tried to get her to give him more details so he had some level of defense.

"What are you talking about? We're always together. He's never by himself." Then before Dakota could continue, Rory added his two-cents worth to the conversation.

"Daddy and I are together all the time. He says I'm a bur on his butt sometimes."

Dakota choked at the sound of his own words being echoed by the child who lived with him. It brought him back to something his grandmother had said with great frequency. *'Little pitchers have big ears.'* It had been a constantly stated wisdom when Dakota and his cousins were spending their typical summer's day at their grandmother's house. He always felt she liked that they kept all the aunts and uncles on their toes and honest.

He smiled at the worker and ruffled Rory's hair. "The things they remember... It's my curse that Rory recalls everything. But you didn't come out to talk about quirky things I've said within his hearing. I'm sure comparing him to a cocklebur was one." He took a deep breath and steadied his frown at Tanya. "You mentioned the complaint wasn't from Linda this time. Who's crabby then? It's probably Mom. Wouldn't that be the perfect ending?"

His gaze caught Tanya's and he found that the woman who rarely showed any emotion seemed harsh. "As you are well aware, the submissions to my office are done anonymously." She paused and gloated at him.

He considered calling her on her obvious bias, but Dakota didn't think antagonizing her was a good idea. He refocused on Ms. Gideon when she spoke again.

"But I can tell you it was not either of the grandmothers. This time it was your own stupidity that caused your problem."

Dakota could visualize her in the role of villain in one of the old black-and-white melodramas. Twirling the mustache might have been overly dramatic, but the character fit her best.

"According to the filed complaints, you left Rory alone in a camper trailer while you were wandering over the rodeo grounds." She checked on the notes in her case file. After a few seconds of searching, she stabbed her finger into the note-covered page.

"Ah yes, I thought there were more details. It seemed that while this was happening, a fire broke out, endangering the entire campground. The complaint was filed by someone who was also staying in the same location, so they had seen you and the child earlier in the week." She ran her finger down the page for a few seconds before closing her book and turning to Dakota.

"If the final decision rested with me, I would place Rory somewhere safe. But when I gave my supervisor my recommendations, she overrode some of my more strongly held opinions."

Dakota shook with the stress of the moment, realizing Rory was crying and clinging to him. Rory's reaction galvanized Dakota's initial response to her threat. "Rory isn't going anywhere unless you have paperwork from a judge. He's had enough bad things happen over the last year. I won't let you traumatize him further because of some personal vendetta you have against me."

Her lips formed a hard line as he waited for her reply. The silent tension between them didn't continue for long.

"The unneeded stress was the point my supervisor wanted to make certain was being addressed. Our focus is on the welfare of the children in our care. Once we are confident they are in the best of care, the needs and desires of any adults are considered."

Dakota measured her for a minute, uncertain how much of that response was the official reply from her boss. He felt it was a carefully orchestrated combination. This was his family she was ready to sacrifice, and he would fight like hell to keep them together. At some point, the fact he was alone with a youngster would rise to the forefront, but at this instant, he focused on his defense. He ramped up his control and refused to antagonize Ms. Gideon.

He lost that battle when he caught the smirk on her face.

"Maybe you should listen to your boss and not harass Rory and me. Personally, I think it's pissing you off that we're doing so well. You never have liked me. You don't think I can take care of Rory. Well, that's fine, because I have no intention of letting go of my parental rights. Not you, not my mother and hell will freeze over before I let Linda Morris take my son."

He knew he had just lost any chance of getting the woman on his side. When he gathered himself and met her gaze, all he saw was a twisted mouth that was a little bigger than a dash and eyebrows that appeared to be trying to climb off her face. Her next words were said only slightly above a hiss as she slapped the envelope from her stack of paperwork onto his chest.

"Were it up to me, Mr. Neri, I would place Rory with a foster family, but as I told you, that option was taken away. So, the court will decide."

Rory understood what was happening and cried again. Tears filled his eyes and ran down his face. They were small and controlled at first, but in seconds they became a waterfall of emotion. He sobbed as he voiced his distress.

"You can't take me away from Daddy. He's taking care of me." Rory's wail approached hysterical when he gasped a chest full of air and continued, "You can't do it. You are a terrible lady if you give me to someone else."

Rory was gathering his breath and thoughts to continue to voice his opinions when Dakota knew this conversation needed to end. He turned to the woman who'd brought on this turmoil. "Ms. Gideon, I'd like for you to leave. You have brought nothing but pain and misery to Rory and me. Our lives may not fit into your idea of what a father and son should be. Of course, I'll be at the hearing, but I hope you discover your empathy before then." He paused for a moment and considered what else he might want to add. "I'm sure you deal with some horrible people. I see it on television all the time. You can't let the few bad ones you work with paint all of us with a broad brush."

He stopped, waiting for her to blast him in bits scattered all the way to Tulsa. Instead, she drew her face even tighter, clenched the paperwork in one hand and marched to the dark SUV. As she left the driveway, she never turned another glance their direction.

By the time she'd disappeared with a cloud of dust trailing her, Rory was down to a few sniffles. He held tight, wrapped his arms around Dakota's leg and squeezed. Dakota gave him time to gather himself. He didn't want Rory to rush to deal with the crisis she had dumped on them. Before long, Rory calmed himself, then drew back to look at Dakota.

"She's mean. I don't like her. She does nasty things."

Dakota considered his words before answering his son. When he did, he kept his comments more generous than his actual opinion. "I don't think she intends to be ugly, but she has a difficult job, and sometimes it doesn't come out the way we want."

Rory studied him for a moment then ask the question Dakota dreaded. "Is she going to take me away?"

"No. She will not take you."

"But that's what she said. She said she was taking me somewhere else and I wouldn't live with you and Papa anymore."

He struggled with the wording of his reply to make the youngster feel better. "She isn't going to take you to a new place. You don't fret about it. I'll take care of whatever needs to happen."

He ruffled Rory's hair and lowered the little boy to the ground. He reached out, took Rory's hand in his and started toward the stables.

"We have lots to do. Let's not worry about Ms. Gideon. We need to take care of the animals." A thought occurred to him that should distract Rory. "Didn't you have a chicken sitting on a nest full of eggs?"

Rory's head snapped up, and a grin covered his face. "Yeah, I think I know where she's hiding it too. Come on. Let's go look."

He grabbed Dakota's hand and started toward an outbuilding at a full run. Dakota grinned from ear to ear, pleased he'd found such a good distraction.

* * * *

Ayden gritted his teeth at the sight of Jordan. He'd hoped that deciding to divert his circuit and go to the Little Rock rodeo would bring him some luck…and peace. From her expression, he would be on the receiving end of yet another ass-chewing. It was getting to the point where his friend needed to stop sharing her view of how all this should be between them. And he was always on the short end of the stick when it was being dished out.

He refused to stand and wait for her like a wayward child. He'd at least have her come to him. So, he made his way to the horse trailer, then led his mare out and into the stall where she would stay while they were taking part in the contest. Ayden checked the halter for his mare then verified the hay and fresh water he'd put into their respective containers a few minutes ago. He turned away as he heard boots coming through the gravel path toward him. He locked eyes with Jordan.

Before she could begin, Ayden held up his hands. "Wait until I finish with the horses to give me your opinion of whatever I did wrong." He waited until he got a nod before turning away. Ayden smiled to himself when the fence creaked as she leaned against it and cleared her throat.

"Nice pair of mares. I thought you only had the one," she said.

Ayden leaned into the brush, causing the horse to make contented sounds. He glanced back at Jordan. "The black one is Midnight. I've been riding her for the last year. This one? Well, we're getting her in shape for Nationals."

Jordan cocked an eyebrow. "We?"

"We."

Both Jordan and Ayden turned toward the new person that neither of them had heard coming. Ayden trotted across the pen, scaled the tubing panel and wrapped Shane in a tight hug. Shane's expression filled with happiness. The embrace lasted a minute before Ayden released him and he turned to Jordan.

"Hey, baby girl. What are you doing here? This is out of your normal route."

Jordan smirked before answering his question. "I came to see Ayden. He and I needed a chat, and I thought it was one better done face-to-face. But running into my favorite West Texas bull fighter doesn't hurt my feelings at all." Jordan leaped at Shane and wrapped him in a tight hug. When she released him, the glance she gave Ayden had more than a note of sadness.

Shane must have recognized the signs of an unpleasant conversation. He waited only a few scant seconds before making an excuse to not be in the area when Jordan unloaded on Ayden for whatever his latest transgression turned out to be.

"I'll check back later. I've got another meeting with a guy out of Florida who needs new herd bulls. It shouldn't take long." He shook everyone's hands and disappeared into the crowd.

Both stood watching until he had melded into the mass of people, then Ayden met her gaze.

"What did I do this time? Nothing I know of, but I'm sure you'll be able to explain why I'm so wrong. So, go ahead. Blast me."

She crossed her arms and frowned at him. The first words out of her weren't what he'd expected, though.

"When are you planning to visit Rory?"

Ayden worked his mouth up and down like a beached fish. *Shit, my day is going to crap.* He met Jordan with a considered level of response. He knew he would have a struggle. Her focus on family was legendary on the rodeo circuit. If she thought Ayden was not giving Rory his utmost care, there would be hell to pay. He tried to gather his thoughts, but she had obviously given this a lot of consideration and he wouldn't win the argument.

"I can't believe you deserted Rory and haven't been back to see him. What were you thinking? You and Dakota play whatever games the two of you want, but if you mess with that boy… I swear you'll regret it."

Ayden bristled at the accusations. "We've been through this already. I didn't do anything to Rory. He's a great kid. But no one talked to me about raising him. Hell, Dakota doesn't even want to get married. Every time it's come up, he avoids the whole conversation."

Jordan cocked one eyebrow. "What about yours and Dakota's open relationship?"

"Where'd you get that idea?" Ayden asked.

Jordan's laugh became more heartfelt. "Because you told me earlier in the summer and it sounded to me that you both enjoyed that arrangement."

Embarrassment washed over him. "Okay. I get your point. It still doesn't let Dakota off the hook for the crap I put up with and how much Rory became my responsibility while Dakota kept working on the rounds at the rodeo. It would be good if he'd talk about all the problems that were his fault."

"So, let me see if I have this rationale of yours narrowed down," Jordan said. "Dakota got Rory dropped on him with only a passing discussion. Then he started roping again, and you didn't like it. Isn't that how he makes a living? Did you talk to him about the things making you crazy? Anything? Even a hint?"

Ayden rolled his eyes but felt a twinge of guilt that made him realize some of what Jordan had said was far too close to factual than what he would have liked.

I wanted to be the long-suffering one, but some of this failing relationship is my fault.

Stubborn to the core, he had no intention of admitting to Jordan that he was part of the trouble. Still, he had to deal with the cowgirl and her accusations.

"Some issues were on me. Regardless, it's too late now. We said unforgivable things."

Jordan made a sound that would have been more recognizable from a mare, but he got the idea that she was not satisfied with the reply Ayden had given her.

"You walked out on a kid who thought of you as his parent. When I saw him, he was asking everyone when you were coming back—like you told him you would. How shitty can you be?"

Ayden frowned as he went through his final conversation with Rory, and he had to admit their separation might not have been handled as well as it could have been. He had promised to visit Rory. The sting was more than he'd bargained for as he turned to Jordan.

"Okay, you're right. I screwed up with Rory. I didn't carry through with what I told him. What I did was crappy. Once I finish the competitions I've already submitted entry fees for, I'll head for Krebs. It's going to take schedule juggling, but it'll happen as soon as possible. I promise."

Jordan stood close, shaking her finger in his face. "Don't forget again. Don't do Rory like my dad did me."

Ayden focused on Jordan's face. It upset him to see the impact his thoughtless action had had on his friend. A single tear leaking from her eye was the ending of any kind of argument about what part of the disaster was clearly his. It didn't matter. He had to fix the problem he'd created.

"I didn't know about your dad. You never talked about him. I won't let that happen with Rory."

With an angry slash of her hand wiping the moisture from her face, she banished all signs of vulnerability to the seventh hell. When she turned back to Ayden, any weakness had disappeared.

"You need to fix this. For Rory's sake, make it right. If you and Dakota can't live together...whatever. If y'all screw with that little boy, you're going to find out what happens when you piss off a girl from the hills of Oklahoma." She lifted her eyebrows as she pressed her lips together hard. "It's a fact too, Ayden. I won't tolerate Rory being hurt any more. I'll come hunting for you and Dakota."

Their eyes locked until Ayden dropped his gaze to the ground. After a minute slipped by, Ayden spoke. "Like I said, I have a couple of rodeos I'm committed to already, but as soon as I take care of those, I'll visit Rory and make sure he's okay."

"Don't think it'll be some quick thing to eliminate your commitment."

"I never—"

Jordan cut him off before he could explain why so many of the things she was spewing didn't reflect his situation. She obviously didn't care about the details of the problems between him and Dakota.

She moved even closer and stabbed a finger into the center of his chest. It always amazed him how she could create such a commanding presence with her full height of five feet two inches.

"Take care of this, Ayden."

With that final command, she spun and disappeared into the crowd. Ayden stood staring at the point where he'd last seen her and tried to plan out what he needed to do. He wasn't going to follow Jordan's orders as a way to placate her, although he didn't mind that as a side effect.

He went back to the horses, retrieved his brush and began grooming them meticulously as he pondered his choices and what he should do to help settle Rory into his new life. It didn't take long before he'd lost himself in options and scenarios.

"If you keep brushing her like that, she'll look like an opossum's tail."

Startled, Ayden jumped in surprise at hearing Shane's voice. A second passed before he remembered Shane had told him he'd come back once he'd settled his other business. Ayden also thought Shane hadn't planned to return until after whatever conflict he was having with Jordan was over.

Ayden stopped what he'd been doing and met Shane's gaze. He gave his friend a shy smile. "I could say she's a new hairless breed from Iceland or something."

Shane chuckled. "If she had a bunch of wrinkles too, she'd be worth a fortune." He stepped closer and leaned against the railing. "So... Do we pretend the mare is what we're talking about or acknowledge the three-hundred-pound gorilla in the room?"

Ayden sighed before putting the curry comb into the grooming box. "I hate to bring it up. I'm sure you don't want to hear my personal crap."

Shane gave Ayden a smile wrapped in a shrug. "You'll obsess about the ass-chewing Jordan just laid on you and won't be listening to me at all if we don't take care of this."

Ayden sighed but nodded the entire time. "Okay. You're right. I won't be able to focus on anything else."

"Mind if I listen in too?"

Ayden groaned and turned behind him to find Shane's husband shooting him a concerned expression. Shane rolled his eyes but wasn't distressed by the new addition as he turned to Ayden. "Hope you don't mind. I figured Dustin could give you a different perspective than me. He has had to live with a whole special set of problems too." He grinned and tugged Dustin close. "Besides, we're both uncles to my nephew. I think he's about the same age as your youngin'. So it's not like we're some kind of childless couple with no experience with kids."

"Come on. Tell us about your hubby issues. We might even help. Lord knows we had enough troubles when we first met," Dustin said.

Ayden looked from one to the other. He knew these guys, but he hadn't considered them close enough to share the mess that had become his life. The more he thought, though, the more it sounded like a decent scheme to get someone else's opinion. It couldn't be any worse than one of Jordan's sessions.

"Okay, sure. Maybe you can give me some suggestions. Otherwise, I'll go back to my current system, which is pouting and feeling put upon."

Dustin chuckled, and Ayden noticed his comment even had Shane smiling. He waved them to the trailer and let them inside. He turned on the lights and motioned to the seats.

"Make yourself comfortable. I've got a few beers from my last rodeo that are decent."

"Sure," Dustin said.

"Sounds like a good plan," Shane added.

Ayden fished out the drinks, popped them open and handed them to his guests. After a swig of his, he settled down into the last open place.

"No use waiting. What'd you want to know?" Ayden asked.

"Start at the beginning. Your drama is never that simple. We can always rein you closer if you're giving us too much detail."

Ayden considered Shane's instructions and nodded. He spent the next half hour going through everything, from how he and Dakota had met to why Rory was in Dakota's care. He stopped, his throat dry from the non-stop narration. Dustin took advantage of the lull to clarify a few details.

"So it was Dakota's ex-wife who created the paperwork for him to be Rory's guardian if something happened to her?"

Ayden swallowed, nodding in agreement. "That's what the sheriff and the caseworker told us. And it didn't seem like his mother-in-law knew anything about it. She was ready to bury Dakota deep in the Ouachita Mountains once she'd done away with him."

Dustin chuckled, his eyes twinkling as he considered the information Ayden shared with him and Shane. Ayden gave them some time before questioning them.

"So what do you think? Jordan was blunt that it was my fault and I should have been more understanding. I was tired of being the mostly stay-at-home parent when my job is to be a winning calf roper too. I'm only twenty-five, for God's sake."

Dustin was still wearing the same smirk. Shane seemed to find it less humorous.

"Shane, what do you think?" Ayden said.

"Well, it sounds kind of familiar. Dustin and I lived through something similar. Part of the argument was over my nephew. My twin brother and his wife wanted a kid, but Sam was shooting blanks. So, I agreed to help."

Dustin made a polite cough and when they gazed his direction, he tilted his head toward Shane.

Shane threw his hands in the air. "Okay. All right. Sam asked me to be the donor for their baby since we're identical twins."

When Shane stopped, Dustin continued the tale. "He's leaving out a few parts, like not wanting to be their donor."

"Too much responsibility? That's how I felt. It's overwhelming," Shane said.

"Actually, I wanted to be more involved, not less. That's where our story gets to be more similar to you and Dakota," Dustin replied.

"How's that?" Ayden asked.

Dustin explained. "I felt like you do now. I didn't want the obligation of a kid. We had at least talked about it before Shane agreed to be the donor, though. The closer the deadline came, the more I worried. It wasn't one of our best times."

Ayden studied each of them. "But now things are just great, right?"

Shane chuckled and reclined in his seat. "Things are fine now, but we had help to get things worked out. First, and most important, Austin is not our child. We were welcome to be doting uncles, but Sam's wife made it clear that she and Sam would be his only parents."

Ayden chuckled at the thought of them being dressed down by the tiny West Texas woman who Sam had married. Like most mothers, she would defend her children to the end. He'd met her on a trip to see a horse Shane was training and had easily determined that he never wanted to cross her.

"Things worked out for the best in our case. We're the most amazing babysitters a kid could ask for."

Ayden focused on Dustin and contemplated the wording of his next question. He aimed it at Dustin. "How did you get over the issues you had with Shane having a child?"

Dustin pursed his lips and stared into space for several minutes before he turned back to meet Ayden's gaze. "It took a while. My ADHD didn't help either. After a few months of me driving Shane crazy with questions and spending time with the little shit, I fell in love with him. From there, Shane and I worked out whatever details we needed between the two of us. Our situation never got as drastic as yours."

Ayden sat for a minute before taking the conversation further. Once he'd considered Shane and Dustin's suggestions, he realized that he needed to change some of his views, especially about Rory.

"I can see what you mean," Ayden said. "Rethink what happened and make sure Rory understands none of our mess is his fault. I'll have things worked out in a few weeks. Then I can swing by home and spend time with Rory."

"And Dakota?" Dustin asked.

Ayden scowled. "We'll see how Dakota's coped with being the sole caregiver."

Shane crossed his arms and cocked an eyebrow at Ayden. "I think we've played helpful older uncles long enough. Let's check the mare and see what suggestions I have."

They had only spent a few minutes inspecting the animal when Dustin popped his head up and met Ayden's glance with a heartfelt expression. "You can still talk to us any time."

At Ayden's lack of response, Shane laughed. "Dustin means feel free to talk to us about anything we can help with—but especially that offer holds true with Rory. That's only because we probably have had similar problems with Austin." Shane gazed first at one of them then the other. "Now, let's concentrate on the mare. She'll be easier to figure out."

Both Dustin and Ayden chuckled and focused on the horse Ayden planned to use to work his way to the National Finals.

Chapter Fifteen

The knock sounded urgent as Dakota raced to answer the door. Part of the reason he hurried was that Rory had fallen asleep and given him a few precious minutes of free time. He loved the kid, but his edges were unraveling with the responsibility of caring for the little guy. Dakota reached the front door just as another flurry of pounding erupted.

He took a second to compose himself so he wouldn't unload on the innocent person who was knocking. Once he thought he could maintain some level of civility, he opened the heavy wooden door. The individual standing on his porch didn't appear any happier to be there than Dakota, but his focus changed more quickly.

"Dakota Neri?"

He nodded. "Yeah, I'm Dakota."

He caught the large manila envelope out of reflex and stared with a dazed expression.

"You've been served."

"Served?"

The fellow hot-footed his way across the yard to the pickup idling just outside the gate. It stunned Dakota as the guy vaulted into the waiting truck, spun it around and left two stripes down the driveway. Dakota closed the door then turned the packet back and forth a few times as his dread became overwhelming.

He stepped to the dining table and laid the package out with care. He eased into the nearest chair and centered the envelope in front of him. Waiting seemed ridiculous. Nothing would change the contents.

He fished out his pocketknife. After opening the longest blade, he slipped it inside the corner of the package and peeled it open with a flick of his wrist. The silence was deafening as he separated the sheets of paper. His blood ran cold as he read what they contained. When he saw the name Linda Morris, he sensed a fist closing around his throat.

He got the basic message. Linda had filed for custody. He'd known it was coming but the reality still hit hard. The more he saw, the tighter the band circling his chest became. The enormity of his situation overwhelmed Dakota. He sat at the table with his fingers intertwined.

"You okay, Daddy?"

Dakota spun to discover Rory standing a few feet away and looking more worried than a child his age should be. Dakota drew his scattered thoughts and tried to put his words into a form that would comfort Rory. "Daddy's fine. I got paperwork I have to take care of before it gets out of hand. It's something I'll deal with. Don't worry about anything."

Rory wiped a tear from Dakota's cheek. "Why are you crying then, Daddy?"

He let the breath he had been holding leak out before trying to give a good answer. "The stuff the man gave me isn't fun, but everything's okay."

Rory watched him with the same intensity that one of the old-timers gave to a new roper on the circuit. It was so out of character that Dakota wanted to chuckle, but he refused to worsen Rory's concern.

Rory said, "I think it's time for Papa to come home. He's been gone long enough, and we need his help. You should call him and tell him."

Dakota almost chuckled at the serious tone of the boy's approach, but he didn't want his son to think his suggestion was being ignored. He studied Rory before answering.

"I'll see if I can find Papa, but I don't know where he is. We'll be fine. I'll take care of things."

He paused for a heartbeat as he considered his options. He decided it wouldn't do any good to get Rory all worked up. Dakota had to distract the boy. It didn't take long to find the diversion he needed. Rory loved the animals and he could spend hours not only caring for them, but talking and petting each one until he'd made them tame as any pets. That was his key to keeping Rory from stressing.

He patted Rory on the cheek. "Let's go see how your new chicks are adjusting. We need to care for the animals before dinner."

Rory's face shone as he took Dakota by the hand. "They're fantastic. I checked early this morning. Everybody was doing well and had eaten what I gave them last night." He paused for a short period before continuing. "They are tiny though. It would be good to check again."

Dakota ruffled Rory's hair. "I think you're right. They're small, and we can see how they are doing."

* * * *

The two weeks since they had served him the court papers seemed to have disappeared. He understood the implications of what Kayla's mother was doing, but nothing was happening in his favor. He'd felt deserted in the whole process. People who should have had his back were not to be found. He trembled as he waited for his turn before the judge.

Dakota feared his pride would be his undoing. He knew his leg was bouncing like a nervous jackrabbit, but it was too late for him to change the poor decisions he'd made. The courthouse clock seemed determined to keep his ordeal from ending. To make the situation worse, Linda and a handful of people who Dakota could only assume were her lawyers were sitting together at the opposite end of the hallway. Dakota wanted to leave, to run somewhere safe where no one would ever find him—at least until Rory was an adult and could make his own choices.

As he was spiraling into a quagmire of fear and anxiety, the heavy doors to the courtroom swung open and Dakota heard the words he was both desperate to hear and dreaded.

"Neri versus Morris."

He turned from Linda and her entourage to keep from a confrontation with her. Dakota knew it was well within her temperament to explode at him during the court proceedings. He stayed behind, holding Rory's hand. The room was dead silent as he walked to the table he'd been motioned toward.

He followed everyone else's example and sat without moving as the judge flipped through the paperwork. Then she slipped off her reading glasses, laid them on the top of the stack and locked her gaze on Dakota. A second or two passed before she asked.

"Mr. Neri, are you planning on serving as your own counsel?"

The question rattled Dakota, and he replied without careful consideration. "No, Ma'am. But I couldn't find a lawyer who would take my case for what I can pay them."

She motioned the guard closer and spoke a few soft words that had the man scrambling. When she turned back to him, Dakota thought he could detect a slight softening of her expression. "I'm assigning an attorney to represent you. The child will also have a representative appointed." A second later, the ring of the gavel filled the courtroom and the judge exited. As he tried to collect his thoughts, he realized Linda was arguing with the people around her. That simple fact gave him the impetus to get out of the building before she changed her focus.

He started for the door when two individuals appeared beside him. Neither of them said a word, but they seemed intent on talking with him. One was a ginger-haired guy and the other was a dark-haired young woman with a soft brown skin tone. The redhead motioned them toward a closed door at the end of the corridor.

"Come with us," he urged and Dakota followed, compelled by the tone in the man's voice.

They hurried down the hallway and Dakota wondered what they were doing as they entered a dark conference room and flipped on the lights. They removed stacks of paperwork from their briefcases and spread them across the table. Giving them time to do whatever it was they were working on, Dakota surveyed the chamber they were using. It was an enormous space, probably well known by the people who needed such facilities. He pulled out the closest chair and sat with Rory on his lap. After a few minutes more, Dakota decided the overwhelming silence was getting on his nerves.

"Hi. I'm Dakota Neri and this is Rory. I'm guessing whatever you're doing has something to do with us?" Dakota cocked an eyebrow as he let his gaze travel from one to the other.

The expression they shot Dakota would have been comical under other situations. "I'm Doug and this is Sharon. We are the public defenders who are representing you and the kid."

Dakota bristled at the wording. "The kid?"

Sharon waved her hand in dismissal. "Doug didn't mean anything by what he said. I'm Rory's attorney, anyway."

Dakota ran his fingers through his short hair as his nervousness worsened. "So you'll be watching out for Rory?"

Sharon bobbed her head. "Yes, sir. It's my job to preserve his rights and try to do everything so that it's in his best interest. We need to start the paperwork so it's processed in time to meet the judge's trial dates. It's not good to miss deadlines from Judge Swiney."

"Okay, so you're the good guys in this situation. Rory and I appreciate that."

His concern grew at the significant glance running between the two before they returned to shuffling forms. He waited for a few seconds, but they weren't sharing whatever caused their apprehension. He decided this was not the time for quiet acceptance.

"What's wrong? That was a serious look that passed between the two of you," Dakota asked.

Sharon drummed her pencil on the table while Doug sat expressionless. She flipped through a few pages and traced her way down the sheet before turning back. "What did you do to make Mrs. Morris hate you so much?"

Dakota flinch but addressed the question as honestly as possible. "She didn't like that her daughter fell for a rodeo cowboy. When we got a divorce and Ayden moved in, her mood regarding me soured from crap to plumb nasty. After Kayla died in the accident..." Dakota shrugged his shoulders in a wordless explanation. "Why? What's the problem? Kayla wanted me to raise Rory, so why is there an issue?"

"Well, the first obstacle is that the court will decide if staying with you is in Rory's best interest. Then there's the firm she hired from Dallas."

Dakota's chest tightened and a bitter bile gathered in his throat. "What's the problem with her lawyers?"

This time Doug joined in the discussion. "She has employed the four horsemen of the apocalypse. That would be the complication. Not only will they likely win but they'll feed your corpse to the jackals at the Fort Worth Zoo."

Dakota shifted his gaze from one grim face to the other. This wasn't going to go as well as he'd hoped. His gut tied into a knot at the real possibility he would lose custody of Rory. That changed everything, at least from his point of view. With this new information, his focus turned toward keeping Rory, even if it was as a single parent.

He came out of his daze to find the attorneys staring at him. After a second or two, determination filled his thoughts. He would fight this as long as possible. He locked eyes with them and nodded.

"What do I need to do to keep my kid?"

Chapter Sixteen

The fading evening sun bathed both Dakota and Rory as Dakota worked at getting them ready for a night at the roping competition. The court had let him keep Rory, pending the hearing, but it was under the condition that Rory had someone watching him when Dakota couldn't be there. So far, the plan to hire teenagers of people he knew from his years on the roping circuit was working. He feared one of them would flake out, but that was impossible to predict. He just tried to have alternative sitters for each time he needed someone. Tonight was a little different. He'd hired a high school senior, which wasn't unusual, but his backup was her boyfriend, one of the teenage bull riders.

"Daddy, who am I going to play with tonight? I want someone fun."

He thought about the way Rory had worded his question. "Are some of them not fun?"

The boy studied Dakota for a few seconds, seeming to realize this question could have long-lasting consequences on everyone involved. He held Dakota's gaze anyway and gave his response. "Most of them are fine, but I don't think some of them like little kids."

Dakota's heart clenched at the words he'd heard coming from his son. Through all this mess, he wanted more than anything for Rory to be spared drama. He shook his head and knew the cramp in his stomach was only going to become worse. He considered how to explain their situation when Dakota's world unraveled yet again.

His phone rang and the name of the girl who had agreed to watch Rory tonight was on the display.

"Hey, Gale. What's up?" Dakota asked.

Her reply came in a series of gasped-out words filled with emotion. "A deer ran in front of Kyle. When he swerved, he hit a tree. He's in critical condition and they're Life Flighting him to Houston. I have to be with him."

A voice inside Dakota wanted to say 'so you and Kyle won't be able to help me tonight then,' but fortunately for his already-sometimes-questionable sensitivity to other people, he stopped himself. An instant later, he managed to say something that sounded like it came from a person with a drop of empathy oozing through his body.

"Of course, Gale. You focus on making sure Kyle recovers as quick as possible." Dakota thought through the situation and made another attempt. "Do you have someone to take you to the hospital? You don't need to make the drive alone."

He could hear the barely contained hysteria in her voice as she answered. "I'm with Kyle's brother. His parents are meeting us at the hospital."

Before the conversation could drag out further, Dakota shut it down. "Be careful, Gale. Take care of that boyfriend of yours."

A sob echoed from the phone just before the connection was cut. By then, Dakota was securely focused in his own issues. There would be a time in the future when he would realize how selfish he had been, and the guilt would make him feel terrible. For now, his immediate problems were the only thing he could focus on, and Rory's next words brought him back to the present.

"Are Gale and Kyle okay?" he considered for a moment and continued. "They were fun sitters. Did they have a wreck? Are they okay?" He swallowed hard and the tears rolled down his cheek. "Mama had an accident..."

He hugged Rory, rocking him as he cried. "You don't worry, baby. Kyle is going to a big hospital in Houston. The doctors will take care of him. You don't worry about it."

Rory snuggled against Dakota and a few minutes later had calmed himself. Dakota rocked Rory and it wasn't long before he had fallen asleep, twitching slightly as Dakota eased him onto the bed. Dakota stepped outside, pacing across the grassless yard as he called everyone who might watch Rory. The stress grew with each passing moment as person after person couldn't help. In his desperation, he considered calling his mother. She would try to bail him out, but he didn't know what she could possibly do from several states away. His panic reached new levels until he was calling people who were friends of friends. He sat on the tailgate of the pickup, went through his list of contacts and realized it was short. Some he didn't trust with his son and others would not make a favorable impression to the court.

What he'd conceived so far all seemed to be leading him to one choice, forfeit his go and head back. But trying to handle the finances alone had left him behind on the mortgage and several other bills. He wanted to hire a better lawyer than the one appointed by the court. The world seemed to be closing around him as he dealt with his problem alone and he discovered he was bad at taking care of himself. It wasn't that he had no skills, but he fell into the category of people who did good to make it from paycheck to paycheck. Ayden was the one who was all about budgets and investing. He'd done all the work to find them the ranch and determined it was within their income. At the time it hadn't seemed like that big a deal. He'd even dismissed Ayden's skill. Now he missed the ease with which Ayden traversed their finances. Just thinking about it made Dakota's stomach roil into a forbidding knot.

"Hey. How are things going?"

The owner of the voice registered with Dakota as Rory ripped past him and threw himself into Ayden's arms. He crawled up the fit man like a squirrel up a tree.

"Papa! Papa, you're here! I knew you'd be back to stay with us."

Dakota wasn't certain how to interpret the glance Ayden gave him, but the affection he gave Rory left no doubt that he'd missed the boy. Rory made it obvious he had no intentions of letting Ayden slip out of his grasp. He had also settled a question Dakota had been wondering about. Ayden wiped tears from both Rory's eyes then kissed his forehead.

"Rory, I'm here for a visit, but I'm not coming back to the ranch — at least not right now. I'm doing pretty well and have a good chance of qualifying for the National Finals Rodeo. You wouldn't want Papa to miss his chance at winning like that, would you?"

Rory developed a stubborn expression that was all too familiar to Dakota. He had no intention of making life easier for Ayden. He also couldn't care less about how Ayden was doing in the finals. His only focus was getting his family back together.

"Papa, I'm glad the roping is going good but I want you to come home. It's time."

Dakota couldn't help but smile as Rory reeled Ayden into his trap. The direction taken by their son was a surprise for Dakota as much as Ayden.

"Grandma Morris wants me to live with her, but we don't want that to happen. The judge is going to make up her mind soon and I may have to go live with Granny."

Dakota could tell the information had come as a surprise to Ayden. *I guess I could have told him. He might have even been able and willing to help me through all the recent crap.* Before Ayden could pepper him with questions, he began recounting the recent events.

"Linda filed for custody. The lawyer assigned to my case… Well, I'm pretty sure this is his first real case. The one they assigned to defend Rory's rights is focused only on him. I have a court order saying the shit will hit the fan if I leave Rory alone again." Dakota waved his hand and dropped his gaze to the ground. "Don't ask, and yes, I can be that stupid. Today was great because the person I had to watch Rory, as well as her boyfriend who was my backup, are on their way to Houston, one of them in a medivac helicopter. I've called everyone close enough to arrive in time but none of them can help."

Ayden cocked an eyebrow. "Let me guess. Everyone told you to go soak your head in the river."

Dakota barked out a rough laugh. "Some weren't that nice about it. Apparently, some of the people I know consider me to be a dick."

This time Ayden's laughter was a magnitude kinder. "I think it would be best if I didn't comment on that topic. I will give you the slack that some of your so-called friends won't."

He turned to the child hiding his face against his chest. "How would you like to stay with me tonight, Rory?" He was quick to repeat his intentions, though, to avoid any misunderstanding Rory might suffer from and added, "I'm not moving back in with your daddy and you. You're right though. I did promise to come back and visit."

A smile grew across Rory's face, even though he seemed to understand this trip had limitations. But he bargained, proving he had no intention of letting Ayden off the hook. "You'll come back again then too. Granny Linda isn't fun to live with. She only wants to sit around and watch TV. I'd rather you could live with me. We could take care of the animals and go on trips together. That would be okay."

Ayden wore a somber expression. "I'm very busy, Rory. Papa is roping and trying to qualify for the National Finals Rodeo. I promise to come back and see you when I can. Just remember that it may not be as often as we'd like." He hugged Rory tighter and whispered into his ear. "Granny Linda scares me too. I'd rather be cleaning up after the chickens than deal with her."

Ayden lowered Rory to the floor and patted him on the back. "Go get your art box. We can create some new pictures for Daddy. I know he wants some new drawings." He glared at Dakota, who was smart enough to keep his mouth shut when his only source of help was the man who was pissed off at him enough to leave.

Dakota sat for a moment, wondering what Ayden would have to say to him, if anything.

Ayden finally spoke. "This doesn't fix everything. Those problems we had before are still there. But since I got here too late to enter, I can help you out." A small smile appeared on Ayden's lips. "Besides, I made a promise to visit with Rory and I have no intentions of breaking it. So go, get ready. Rory and I will create new artwork for you."

Dakota considered his options carefully before he replied. "That sounds good to me. Maybe I could take us all out for a burger afterward." He paused again and gathered his wits. "Once we get Rory settled into bed, I'd like to talk about you coming home. Would you be willing to discuss it?"

Ayden studied Dakota until he became worried. Before the tension became unbearable, Ayden nodded in agreement. "Okay, but don't get your hopes up. Things have been going downhill for a long time and a few beers over the campfire aren't going to make it all better."

Dakota nodded, but before he had the time to fuck up all his positive work, Rory's voice came from inside. "Daddy, Papa, I have the art box."

Dakota grinned and motioned Ayden to the table where Rory had everything ready for what felt like the first family activity they had shared in months. "You first. Rory has missed you helping him with his art. I'm a sorry substitute."

Ayden rolled his eyes but settled down to the table and started arranging the supplies.

Chapter Seventeen

Ayden curled into the corner and watched as Dakota talked with Rory while he got him ready for a nap. It was like seeing a reflection of the way his parents had treated him at a similar age.

Dakota seemed to have changed but Ayden couldn't bring himself to trust that the changes were permanent. He enjoyed the comfortable sensations of family with Dakota and Rory. He missed the feelings of wellbeing when Rory got tucked into bed with a kiss on the forehead. He had a warm fuzzy sensation when Dakota closed the door and sat beside him.

"You're settling into the whole fatherhood thing pretty well," Ayden said.

Dakota chuckled. "It's working better. It was rough right after…"

Ayden cocked an eyebrow and finished Dakota's sentence. "After I wasn't around to help anymore."

He thought for a minute that Dakota might try to avoid blame. Dakota surprised him. "You're right. I took advantage of you caring for Rory. It gets to be overwhelming. I wish you were with us all the time."

"Did you want me around to sit with your kid or because you missed me?" Ayden asked.

There was a brief pause before Dakota replied. "I suppose both, if I were being honest."

That answer was more candid than he'd expected.

"Okay, at least you're truthful. What's wrong that you are so worried?"

Dakota seemed evasive for a few seconds then exhaled in a gust of frustration. "I left Rory alone for a second in the RV a month back. Someone turned me in to DHS. You know the caseworker is not a fan of mine. So, long story short, if I screw up keeping him safe, I'll never see him again. Of course, there is the whole problem with Kayla's mother, who wants to take Rory away from me."

Dakota shook his head at Ayden then motioned toward the bedrooms. Rory was listening in on the conversation.

A second later Ayden shrugged. He motioned to the child. "Come on, Rory. You can join the crowd."

The barely cracked door flew open and Rory raced across the room to bury himself in the blankets. Before Ayden could ask more questions, Rory lifted his head from where he'd nestled against Ayden. "I don't want to live with Granny Linda. She's scary."

Ayden waited before continuing. He needed to answer Rory. "You'll stay with Papa when Daddy ropes tonight. When the roping ends, we'll have a great night, starting with a big ole funnel cake covered with powdered sugar. Then we'll ride the Sneaky Snake until we're both ready to puke. How does that sound?"

When he spoke, it tore at Ayden. "Can we watch Daddy too? I like seeing him rope."

"We can do whatever you want. I'm sure Daddy would love to have us in the stands and we'll have a great time." He turned to Dakota, filled with long-absent emotions. "Do your best. We'll be cheering you from the grandstands and want to see you win. Got it?"

Dakota grinned at them. "I'll give you something to be proud of. Don't pig out on funnel cake and we can go out for food after I finished."

Rory sat up and chanted, "Corny dogs! Corny dogs!"

Ayden laughed at the kid's enthusiasm. Then he tried to calm him down so the people around them didn't complain. "Okay, bud. Keep it down to a dull roar. You're going to have plenty of stuff happening tonight, including eating too much. Let's see what you pulled out from your art box and let Daddy get ready."

He shooed Dakota into the bedroom then led Rory to the table. Rory set the pace for their activities and it wasn't long before Dakota slipped out. He knew it would be at least an hour before the roping events started, so he gave Rory all the time he needed. From the songs the boy hummed to himself, Rory was enjoying the attention. Ayden let another thirty minutes pass before getting Rory ready for what seemed to be a busy and fun evening.

"Come on, Rory. We need to get your funnel cake now so we aren't late for the competition."

Rory nodded and cleaned up. Ayden watched as everything disappeared into their cubbies. The last of the supplies were stored in short order and Rory tugged on a jacket—all while talking nonstop.

"Tonight will be great. Daddy's good but I wish you were around more. We had a lot of fun before you left. Right now…Daddy's busy, I guess."

Ayden listened for a minute before deciding he needed to give Rory a more holistic view than one where Dakota was the bad guy. So when Rory stopped for a breath, he stepped into the discussion. "Daddy is busy and trying to take care of you the best he knows how. I think he's doing a good job, don't you?"

Rory's face twisted in thought but his reply left Ayden with a smile. "Daddy's great."

Ayden chuckled as they rounded the corner to the aisle with the greatest density of food trucks. He gave Rory's hand a squeeze and swung him onto his hip as they stopped at the order window. While they waited, Ayden continued their conversation. "Did you want to say anything else about Daddy?"

Rory studied him for a few seconds before continuing. "I don't want to upset Daddy…"

"He'll be fine. What's worrying you?"

Rory cupped his hands around his mouth and leaned in to whisper to Ayden. "Life was more fun when you were home with us. It stresses Daddy. It was better when you were there."

A ripple of sadness worked its way through Ayden's system. The maturity of Rory's reply took him by surprise. But he couldn't change how he felt about Dakota. The situation seemed to have improved since he'd left, but some parts needed more progression. So he had to share the truth of his relationship with Rory's daddy.

"Rory, we have a lot of fun when we're all together too. Your daddy and I still need to talk about adult stuff. No matter what happens between your daddy and me, I will always be there for you. Do you understand?"

Rory studied Ayden as if he were a bug he liked. It continued for several seconds before Rory spoke again. "But you're going to come back?" He considered for a few moments. "And more often than last time."

He lifted Rory higher and kissed his cheek. "I promise. I'll see you more. I'll even give you my phone number so you can call me whenever you want. How would that be?"

Rory beamed at him before returning the kiss. "I'd like that a lot."

"Okay, I'm glad that's settled. Now, let's get your funnel cake and go watch Daddy."

He nodded and bucked on Ayden's hip. "Yeehaw! That's really good."

* * * *

The sun had disappeared by the time everything had ended except the midway rides. With the lights and sounds behind them, they arrived at the camper with Rory asleep in Ayden's arms. Dakota unlocked the door and motioned the pair inside ahead of him.

Ayden stood holding Rory and asked, "Where did you want me to put him?"

Dakota gestured toward the front. "Just roll him into a bed. He's definitely Kayla's kid. He wouldn't wake up through an earthquake."

Ayden chuckled as he tucked Rory into the bed. He eased the door shut and returned to find Dakota digging through the refrigerator. "You busy? I could get us a couple of beers…if you're staying for a while," Dakota said.

He glanced around the room before slipping into a seat. "Sounds good. What do you have?"

Without straightening, he handed Ayden a bottle of beer glazed with condensation. "Here. Have a cold one to get you started."

Ayden took the bottle and the opener Dakota handed him. He lifted off the cap with a satisfying pop, scooted into a corner of the table and had a healthy gulp. The chilled liquid eased through Ayden. It was a tasty brew, not the crappy stuff Dakota'd had before. He took another sip and found he enjoyed the taste.

"This is good. When did you stop buying the cheap shit and get something decent to drink?"

Dakota set out a plate filled with different cheeses and a few kinds of crackers. After their evening on the midway, he wasn't all that hungry, but a snack seemed in order to Ayden. After he'd tried a few slices, he let out a sigh and nodded toward Dakota. "That is damn good cheese. A nice snack after all the fair junk."

He glanced over when he heard laughter coming from Dakota. Ayden shot him a questioning expression.

"What?"

"Did Rory wear you out tonight?"

Ayden took a bite of food and made Dakota wait for a reply until he'd swallowed.

"I've eaten enough sweets to give me a sugar buzz. It was worth it though, so Rory could enjoy watching you rope. He thought you should have won too, but he was okay with second. And those corndogs we got after the roping needed something that wasn't fried to go along with them."

"Glad my results kept him happy," Dakota said as he ate.

The contents of the platter disappeared in minutes and they spoke little as they finished their meal. As Ayden leaned against the wall, he noticed Dakota grinning as he slid off his boots and socks. Then he slipped a foot up Ayden's calf.

The contact made him jump and heat rushed through his body. He struggled to gather his wits. When he didn't speak, Dakota shifted his toes higher and rubbed his thigh. Ayden jumped again. This time the caress forced a squeak from his lips, quickly followed by a moan.

"What are you doing? Rory's in his bed and could wake up if we start something."

This time Dakota said nothing but rubbed the ball of his foot over Ayden's package, causing him to wriggle against the cushion and spread his legs wider as the waves of desire swept over him. As much as he lusted for more of Dakota's touch, he wasn't certain he wanted to open that can of worms.

"Dakota?"

The smile on Dakota's face grew. "Yes, Ayden?"

"I don't know…"

Dakota stepped closer, grabbed Ayden's crotch and fondled him. He knew all of Ayden's pleasure points and it seemed he wanted to explore them again. The caress forced a sigh from Ayden.

"I don't know. Sex never suffered while we were together. Do we want to drag it up?" Ayden asked.

Dakota leaned closer and cupped his hands around Ayden's face. The cool sensation felt wonderful on Ayden's skin. When their lips met, it seemed as if a thousand volts passed between them, hitting every erogenous spot on Ayden's body. The strongest sensations raced through his nipples and left him gasping. A few seconds after the caress, Ayden's cock became a granite column. Their kiss stretched for a delicious moment until Dakota drew away, panting for breath.

When Dakota slid his gaze over Ayden, he had a hungry expression Ayden hadn't seen in a long time. He wouldn't mind reliving some of those previous times of intimacy. His days of celibacy could become a distant memory so far as Ayden was concerned. He slid into the booth beside Ayden and ran his fingers across the sexy stubble covering his boyfriend's face. The sensations left Ayden tingling and wanting more. He unsnapped the first two buttons of Dakota's shirt, slipped his hands inside and rubbed his fingers over the light fur. After a few minutes, he caressed the back of Dakota's neck. He drew them close, bringing their foreheads together.

"I've missed your touch. It's been too long, and I'd forgotten how good it feels," Ayden said.

Dakota leaned in and pressed his lips against Ayden's neck. As Dakota shifted lower, Ayden's breathing became heavier. He decided this could go on as long as possible. He pulled Dakota into a gentle kiss.

"Let's move this to the bedroom. I'd like to have lots of doors and even more space between us and your son," Ayden whispered.

"*Our* son," Dakota corrected.

Ayden responded with a nod. "*Our* son. Still, I don't want Rory walking in on us."

Without another word, Dakota pulled him into the bedroom. He locked the door before turning back to Ayden. Ayden sat on the mattress and tugged Dakota to him. They wrapped their arms around each other, caressing with slow, heat-soaked touches. Ayden was ready for the renewal of the physical part of their relationship.

Their foreplay made Ayden hornier with each passing moment and Dakota obviously felt the same. Before long, they were writhing across the bed from wall to wall. The flush of lust engulfed Ayden until he found himself beneath Dakota's muscular torso.

He nibbled down Dakota's neck, enjoying the tastes he found. He bit lovingly over Dakota's ear then whispered. "Damn, you make me randy. You're one of the hottest men I've ever been with."

They managed to strip to their briefs and Ayden had his man firmly pinned. Ayden rubbed and teased Dakota's cock through the tightly stretched material.

"I'll finish in a few seconds if you keep that up," Dakota warned.

Ayden lifted his head and gave Dakota a lecherous grin. "I seem to remember someone who could recharge in a few minutes."

Ayden groaned when Dakota twisted and scraped his teeth over a delightful spot. He ran his hands over Ayden, reveling in the smooth, hard muscles.

"Ah, fuck. This is so good. I love being reminded what being a horny fucking teenager was like," Ayden said.

Dakota crawled over the bed and slid his bare chest across Ayden. The gentle scrape of his short hair against Ayden's smooth skin was enough to keep Ayden on the brink.

Dakota smirked at him as he again crept lower, leaving a trail of kisses until he reached Ayden's briefs. He closed his teeth over the strands of hair that escaped. After more playful teasing, he slipped a finger under either side of the underwear and eased them down Ayden's body. His rock-hard cock pressed against the material as it went lower. The base of his dick appeared as the thin fabric stretched for a moment before popping loose. With a few tugs, the last of Ayden's clothing hit the floor.

Dakota turned back to look at him with an expression of pure desire as he hovered over Ayden's stiff shaft. After a few seconds passed, Dakota dropped lower and took the head of Ayden's dick inside his mouth. The wet heat was almost more than Ayden could take as he edged closer to coming. Dakota circled his tongue around the head of Ayden's cock, pressing harder as the length of his shaft sank deep into Dakota's throat. He worked Ayden's dick until a thick strand leaked from its tip. It wasn't long before Ayden was close to exploding.

The pleasure surging through him stopped when Dakota slipped away.

"Oh holy hell. Why did you stop? It felt so good," Ayden whined.

Without a word, Dakota moved to one side and stripped before dropping back to the bed. He sat on Ayden's chest, took his cock and rubbed it over his lover's face until it was coated with precum. With that, Dakota slipped his hard shaft into Ayden's mouth and he ran his tongue over it like a newborn calf. It didn't take long before Dakota clamped his hands onto Ayden's shoulders, trembling with the force of his pleasure.

Ayden ran his fingers over Dakota's body as he drove his thick shaft into Ayden's throat. Dakota braced himself against the wall and drove faster until a stream of sweat ran over his skin. Ayden reached for the muscular ass pumping above him and caressed it with renewed fervor. He ran his fingers through Dakota's hairy thatch until he located the object of his search.

He pulled free, grabbed a bottle of lube from the nightstand and a few seconds later had the tip of his finger covered with clear gel. Ayden took Dakota's shaft between his lips again then located Dakota's hairy opening and buried his coated finger inside. Dakota trembled, and Ayden knew he had reached his limit. With a low groan, Dakota shuddered, and a second later, the first shot of cum filled Ayden's mouth.

The delight continued as Dakota fed Ayden streams of musky cum. He lost himself in the sensations and scents until he melted into overwhelming longing. Seconds rolled past until Dakota strained a last time, moaned and rolled off to sink onto the mattress. While Dakota panted from exhaustion, Ayden spooned behind him and rubbed his leaking cock over the cleft of Dakota's butt, getting it slick and wet.

As Dakota returned from his euphoria, he began meeting Ayden's thrusts. A few passes over Dakota's opening and Ayden slipped inside with a moan. Ayden pressed deeper until Dakota squirmed under him and Ayden ground his crotch against his man. The delicious sensations wrapped around him as he enjoyed Dakota's tight butt. He leaned low and sank his teeth into Dakota's shoulder.

Dakota muttered, "Ah, yeah. Love your cock. Pound my ass like a bitch."

Ayden froze and there was an extended silence before he laughed. It didn't take long before he sagged beside Dakota as he tried to recover. After a few seconds, he could speak again, and he chanced a look at Dakota. The sour expression plastered across his face almost set Ayden off again.

"You finding something amusing? You're picking a fucking strange time to find that sex with me tickles your funny bone," Dakota said.

"Well? Yeah, you cracked me up. What did you expect when you said *'pound my ass like a bitch'*?"

Dakota squirmed against Ayden, clearly showing he was ready for more, but he managed a stumbling explanation. "Okay, whatever. Maybe I've been watching too much bad porn. Now, can you get back to business?"

Without more discussion, Ayden grabbed his ass and plunged his shaft into Dakota until his bush ground against his butt. He rotated his hips until Dakota seemed lost in the sensation. As Ayden neared the edge of pleasure, his elation grew. He hammered his hips faster until he shook, the orgasm inching closer.

Ayden knew in scant seconds he would empty himself. A few gasping breaths later, his body tensed and Ayden shot deep inside his former lover. The ripples of euphoria rolled over him until his muscles locked with a final convulsion.

Time passed and Ayden cooled as the sweat dried on his skin and his cock softened. He spooned behind Dakota, inhaling the mingling of their scents. Dakota groaned and turned toward him, kissed the tip of Ayden's nose then relaxed. Ayden wrapped his arms around the cowboy and cuddled even tighter. They held each other for what seemed like hours. The chill of the night proved to be too much, however, and Ayden peered at Dakota with a teasing grin.

"My butt's colder than a witch's tit. Let's clean up and get some sleep. Rory gets up way too early for us to stay like this."

Dakota leaned in and gave Ayden a lingering kiss. His eyes twinkled, and he pushed Ayden ahead of him and smacked his ass.

"Start moving or it will be daylight and we'll be dodging questions from Rory."

"That's the last thing I want right now. That kid is too smart for his own good sometimes."

Chapter Eighteen

Dakota turned off the engine and sat staring at the dash of his pickup, overwhelmed by the strength of his emotions. He'd been dreading this day since they'd paraded into court what seemed to be months ago. He'd toed the line since that had happened, but their court-appointed lawyers had brought him even less confidence in the possibility of success than he'd had at the beginning. Now he was questioning his choices and wondering if he wouldn't have been better served to ask his family for assistance. Now the time had come for their reappearance in court and the judge's ruling. The past week had been a storm of legal debris. Unfortunately, his representative had been buried under the constant official tidal wave bearing down on him and Rory that had been brought by the Fort Worth lawyers. As he reviewed the cascade of legal maneuvering they had suffered through, he heard Rory.

"Daddy, you okay?"

Dakota gathered his thoughts so whatever answer he gave Rory was true but wouldn't frighten him.

"I'm okay, Rory. There are just a lot of things happening today. Everything will be fine. Once today's over, all this will be behind us." He thought for a few seconds then added, "Once we're finished this morning, how about we get some ice cream?"

A smile spread across Rory's face. "Chocolate? Can I have chocolate? It's my new favorite."

"You bet! One dish of chocolate for you as soon as this is over."

He released Rory from his booster seat and the youngster scrambled into the front. He spent a minute checking Rory's clothing. The kid sported his summer cowboy hat, pressed jeans and shirt and newly polished boots. He'd intentionally dressed the two of them to look like the ideal father-and-son cowboy combination. No normal human being could possibly see Rory and not make those sounds everyone made over an adorable child.

He dropped to one knee in front of Rory and brushed at imagined motes of dust. A short time later, Rory touched his fingers to Dakota's face. "What's wrong, Daddy? Why are you crying?"

Dakota wiped at his eyes with the sleeve of a shirt pressed until it could stand alone. With a sniffle to give him a moment of recovery, he forced a smile.

"I'm just being selfish. I want to have you all to myself."

Rory wrapped his arms around him and held on tight. It went on long enough that Dakota's concerns got the better of him. He saw his court-appointed lawyer headed toward the courthouse at a fast walk. Dakota swept Rory into his arms and ran after him.

"Doug. Hey, Doug!" Dakota called.

His pace didn't slow, which told Dakota that the lawyer didn't want to be forced into a conversation. But Dakota had no intention of letting him avoid an unpleasant beginning to what was going to be a miserable day. He broke into a dead run and sprinted across the distance separating them.

When they were within a few steps of each other, he called out again. "Doug, hold up."

This time he couldn't avoid Dakota. He dropped back to a normal pace then stopped and turned. "Morning, Mr. Neri. How are you?"

"Shitty as hell. Unless you have some good news that I haven't heard yet."

The long sigh that followed told Dakota far too much. "Nothing's changed. They made the same offer..."

This time Dakota's anger grew faster than a summer grassfire. "The same offer? The fucking ridiculous, piece-of-shit, moronic offer as before?"

"Daddy—"

Damn! I can't let this spill into Rory's world any more than is absolutely necessary.

"Sorry, Rory. Daddy shouldn't use bad words."

He turned back to Doug. "Are we ready for what's going to happen today?"

He sighed again. "Like I said before, she hired a bunch of sharks, and they can smell blood in the water."

"What the —?" He glanced at Rory and saw he was watching closely. He started again. "I don't like to lose."

"I've noticed that. I plan to do my best."

They stared at each other for too long to be comfortable before turning back to the courthouse, making their way past security and to the waiting area. They chose a fairly secluded spot, hoping to avoid a confrontation with Linda and her cadre of lawyers. It didn't help that Doug paced the floor like a nervous border collie. Dakota's heart sank at the way things were falling into place. He had developed hatred for the building and the people who worked inside it. He knew without a doubt that today would be seared into his memory — and not for any positive reasons. He was going to lose custody of Rory.

He realized one of the barracudas had found her way to his tiny refuge and was studying him. When she leaned closer, Dakota recoiled from her proximity. Then he heard a low purr that had to be her voice.

"Give up the fight and give Mrs. Morris custody of the kid. I'll make sure you get visitation." She shot a predatory smile at Rory before turning back to Dakota. "Think of the freedom. What thirty-year-old doesn't relish his time? I'm sure it wouldn't hurt your love life either. I understand your last boyfriend left you because of your private life."

Rory tensed in his arms and shifted away from the woman with the same fear he'd show a diamondback rattlesnake. His intuition said something important to Dakota. He steeled his nerves and fixed a steady gaze on the attorney crouched over them.

"Rory is staying with me. I don't lose."

The smile on her face sharpened. "Judging by the band of cowboys you associate with, this shouldn't take very long."

"Maybe I shouldn't have left my dad's plumbing business. I'd probably be making more money and have more fun," Dakota heard from nearby.

He turned to find Doug standing close with a wistful expression on his face while Rory's representative, Sharon, stood to his side. He heard the lack of confidence his lawyer had in his case. He reached out and patted Doug's shoulder.

"We haven't lost yet."

The rest of the morning was spent playing mind games among all the people involved with the trial. By the time they filed into the courtroom, Dakota was numb and ready to put Doug back on the bus home with instructions for his dad to teach him the plumber's trade. He wasn't certain Sharon was any better, but she certainly wasn't worse. The four of them settled in for a long battle, which Dakota was convinced would be the worst day of his life.

As time crawled by during the hearing, Dakota wondered more and more who they were describing to the judge. They made him sound like some immature and dangerously incompetent person who no one in their right mind would let care for a child. Hell, he wouldn't trust the man they were describing, and it was him.

Any time Doug attempted a legal maneuver, he was obliterated by one of the other attorneys. *The bloodbath is impressive. Too bad it isn't in my favor.* By the time the arguments in favor of Linda were winding down, Dakota wanted to drop his head to the table and cover it with his arms. Then he heard what sounded like the closing discussion. That was the point when he knew his options were gone.

He locked his gaze on the judge and cleared his throat. Once he was certain he had her attention, he spoke. "Your Honor, can I say something?"

She studied him until Dakota thought she would reject his request. Then she sighed and nodded. "Yes. If you have something to add to this case then please do so."

Dakota nodded, gathered his thoughts and went through the past months. He started out presenting his point of view in a cohesive narrative. The hum of conversation grew and his focus disintegrated as he heard a loud voice coming closer. A few seconds later the door burst open and a small army of people rushed into the courtroom. A woman, who seemed like a person not to be trivialized, stood and nodded toward the judge. "My apologies, Your Honor. We have been hired to represent Mr. Neri. We would like to ask for a recess to speak with our client."

The judge studied the three lawyers with the same intensity as Dakota. He knew nothing about the people who claimed to represent him and were dressed in clothing far past his budget limits. His attention shifted back to the proceedings when the judge hammered her gavel a few times and announced, "Court is in recess for one hour, at which time we will reconvene and I will make my ruling."

* * * *

Dakota followed the woman who had carried Rory from the courtroom. When he had tried to ask questions, she had motioned him into silence, letting him know there were better places for that conversation. He walked across the dim room and realized it was not empty. As the space filled and the lights flickered to life, Dakota froze in place.

Around the far end of the table sat three people. One was obviously the lead attorney but the other two rattled Dakota to his core. On the left side of the table sat Ayden. They had met a few times recently to keep his promise to Rory, but that was as far as their conversations had taken them. From his expression, he was an eager participant in the rescue party.

But Ayden's participation wasn't the biggest surprise. That honor was given to his mother, who was seated on the left. Judy Neri left no doubt that she was pleased to be involved in saving her son's life. She was clearly the heroine in this story. At this point, he didn't even care. His world was falling apart, and if his mother could save him and Rory, he'd willingly be in her debt. He sighed and collapsed into the chair across from them. The room exuded the feeling of victory which had been missing from his world for the last few weeks. When it became evident all they intended to do was smile at him, he knew he was going to be forced to begin this conversation.

"Not to be unappreciative about you bringing the cavalry riding in to save me, but what's going on? I haven't heard from either of you recently."

His mother and Ayden exchanged fleeting glances before turning back to Dakota. Then, to his surprise, Ayden began to speak. "After we saw each other a little while back, I tried to find some way to keep you from losing Rory."

Dakota had to smile when his mother cut into the short explanation Ayden had begun. "He wasn't having much luck thinking of solutions. But the summer rodeo started in Rapid City and I thought I might be able to find you and Rory. But instead, I ran into Ayden. We sat down and he filled me in on the case filed against you."

Ayden jumped into the conversation. "I couldn't think of anything to do, but then it came to me — the piece that I'd been missing. I couldn't believe I had been so stupid for so long."

"I was as shocked as Ayden when he told me. I don't trust anyone, but I overlooked that whole angle," Judy said.

Dakota threw up his hands when they both stopped for a second. "What the heck are you talking about? What was so important that everyone missed?"

Everyone in the room broke into soft chuckles about the time he realized one of the lawyers had taken Rory out of the room. That revelation worried and relieved Dakota at the same time. He turned his focus to Ayden and cocked his head.

"What did you figure out that everyone else had overlooked?"

The grin crept back across Ayden's face. "Simple. He's yours."

Dakota knew there was something he wasn't getting. He shook his head slowly then shrugged. "Sorry, babe, but I'm not catching what you're pitching. Use small words and short sentences."

Ayden got that faraway expression he wore when collecting his thoughts. After a few seconds, he tried again. "Rory is *your* son — not your adopted son, your biological son, the child you had with Kayla. She didn't have another boyfriend after you. The timing — "

Dakota held out a hand to stop Ayden. "No, she said the pregnancy was from the one-night stand she had. It can't be me."

Dakota's mother stepped in. "We knew you wouldn't believe us, and besides, the judge needed proof. So, we did a paternity test to prove our idea."

"How? I didn't give you a DNA sample."

"Baby, it's better to compare the parents, but testing with a grandparent is accepted in court these days."

"What about Rory? How did you manage to get a sample from him?"

This time one of the attorneys spoke up. "The last time Ayden watched Rory for you, he got the boy to play 'doctor' and do a cheek swab. We used that for the examination. The court will repeat the testing but we should have enough with this new evidence to keep Rory with you."

Dakota studied each of the people in the room, his mouth opening and closing as he tried to form words. Then what he'd been dreading all day happened. He broke into tears. He dropped his face into his hands as the sobs racked his body. He heard chairs scrape across the floor but couldn't bring himself to find the source.

Arms wrapped around him and he opened his eyes to see his mother and Ayden encasing him in tight hugs. The shock jolted Dakota back to reality. He wrapped his arms around them and they all held each other. In less time than he would have preferred, one of the lawyers stood at the door.

"Sorry to interrupt, but the judge is calling us back into court."

Judy pulled a stack of clean handkerchiefs from her handbag and dried her eyes while handing one to each of the men. As she finished drying her face, she shot them a grin. "I wasn't sure how today would go, but I knew handkerchiefs would be needed either way. Let's go get this cleared up."

They filed into the courtroom and Rory crawled into Dakota's lap. When Ayden sat beside him and took his hand, he felt a relief that had been missing for too long.

Court began, and the new evidence was presented by the lawyers his mother had obviously hired. They went through the new details and he had no trouble reading the emotions of his opposition. As the case droned onward, Linda became closer to hysterical. By the time the judge dismissed her case, her voice was so high it should have broken glass.

His mother spoke with his lawyers before walking over and joining the three of them. Dakota started talking before she could begin. "Mom, thank you for bailing us out. I don't know what I would have done without you. I'll never forget what you did today."

Judy shook her head and laid her arms over the pair's shoulders. "It wasn't just me. I have to give Ayden credit for realizing Rory was your son. I'm thrilled we got it taken care of."

Dakota nodded slowly as he locked his gaze on his mother. He inhaled deeply then sighed. "I can't take Rory away from her. I don't want to do to her what she was trying to do to me. She already lost a child. I couldn't be the one to take away her grandson too."

His mother stared at him for a few seconds then nodded. "It's your decision, son. I have to admit I don't know if I would be that generous."

Judy leaned close and kissed Dakota on the forehead. A second later she was wiping off the lipstick and chuckling. She paused for an instant, nodded sharply then began. "I have a crowd of old friends from A&M who are in Dallas for the weekend. I thought you could use some quiet time. I'll be back on Monday and we can celebrate then. How does that sound?"

Dakota squeezed Ayden against him before grinning at his mother. "That would be great. I know Rory and I are wiped out."

"Sounds like a good idea to me too," Ayden said. "Some sleep and a few days of down time would be great."

* * * *

Ayden drifted awake as the morning sun flooded the bedroom. After a few days to recover, the three of them had begun feeling like a family again. The past night had been the first that Rory hadn't snuck into bed between them. Today, Ayden woke spooned against Dakota with each of them clad only in a pair of underwear. He slipped out and heard Rory snoring from the opposite side of the house.

Ayden locked the bedroom door behind him. He didn't want a sleepy youngster bursting into their room while he and Dakota were having adult time.

Once he'd completed his morning rituals, he slipped back under the sheet with Dakota. He moved closer to his boyfriend until Dakota was wrapped in his arms.

Dakota sighed and stretched before turning so he was face-to-face with Ayden. "Morning, sunshine. How is our child this morning?"

"Snoring as loud as his daddy."

Ayden luxuriated in Dakota's heat as he pressed his lips softly against the dark stubble coating his face. The prickly sensation sent waves of pleasure through him, leaving no doubt about what he hoped would happen next.

Dakota twisted under the sheet and cradled Ayden's head in his hands. He flicked his tongue across the slight opening in Ayden's lips, paused for a second then drove it deep inside his mouth.

Ayden flicked the bedding off and licked his lips at the delicious sight of Dakota's almost-naked body, then eased across Dakota and let out a sigh as they ground against each other. After a few minutes of enjoyment, Ayden slipped lower, taking Dakota's nipple between his teeth and biting until Dakota yelped.

He sat on Dakota's stomach and toyed with his nipples. As he teased his man, he felt Dakota's thick dick against his ass. He enjoyed the hesitant exploration until Ayden was ready to take their pleasure to another level. He kissed between Dakota's pecs before working his way down his man's flat stomach. Ayden reached his navel and gnawed at the thick hair surrounding it. He licked and tugged until Dakota's movements became frantic and his breath was coming in gasps.

Then, through the sounds of desire, Dakota gasped, "Damn. Come on. Do it or I'm going to bust a nut."

Ayden licked Dakota's cock for a few seconds then released it. "What's wrong, big boy? You not getting lucky lately?"

Dakota growled before sticking his tongue out at Ayden and tugging off his briefs. He grabbed his distended member and shook it at Ayden. "You have a child wrap himself around your leg and see how lucky you get."

Ayden grabbed Dakota's sac and gave it a tug. "Were you shopping around for someone to share your bed?"

He squirmed, teasing Ayden, before answering with a wink. "Of course not. I was more interested in saving our relationship than trying to create a new one with someone else." He cocked his head and considered

Ayden. "But what about you? You were fooling around with Kit."

Ayden cocked an eyebrow. "That never happened, and besides, Kit's focused on things other than seducing me. It doesn't hurt that I'm ahead of him in the earnings."

Dakota grinned and climbed onto the bed. "I plan to have sex with the overall winner of the National Finals."

Ayden slid off the bed to step out of his briefs before bounding back beside Dakota and taking him in a passionate kiss. Then he asked, "What did you have in mind?"

Dakota shot Ayden a particularly lecherous glance before saying, "I want to rim your bubble butt until you're begging for more."

Ayden crawled to Dakota and positioned his ass over Dakota's face. Dakota pulled his butt cheeks apart then flicked his tongue over Ayden's hole. The sensation filled Ayden as Dakota flicked his tongue across it over and over again. His head swam as Dakota penetrated deeper. The sensation built as he became wet and loose.

Dakota rolled him to his hands and knees, moved behind Ayden and devoured his ass. He continued until Ayden's muscles felt like gel. Ayden bucked back against Dakota as his desires reduced him to nothing more than an animal in heat. As the tip of Dakota's tongue went deeper yet, Ayden teared up with pleasure. Though his words were lost in his haze of lust, he begged for release. "Fuck me. Fuck me hard. I need screwed," Ayden moaned.

Dakota slapped Ayden on the butt. "You ready for a pounding?"

The sting of the smack curled through Ayden and left him wanting more.

Unable to respond with more than a sigh, Aiden stroked his cock as he spread across the bed. Dakota snagged the bottle of lube from the side table and smeared a wad of the clear gel over his vein-covered dick then over Ayden's hole. Ayden gasped and shuddered as the chilled lubricant coated his asshole. His pleasure expanded as Dakota slid a thick finger inside him.

His feeling of euphoria crested when Dakota slid across his prostate. The electric tingles that raced through his system were like nothing he'd experienced before. His cries reached a volume that forced Dakota to put a hand over his mouth and whisper into his ear.

"Shh, you'll wake Rory."

Ayden buried his face into the pillow as Dakota finger-fucked him. Stretching Ayden to two, then three fingers sent him past the stinging pleasure into the stratosphere. He was reduced to a quivering mass when Dakota slipped his fingers out and grabbed Ayden by the hips.

He ran his cock over his lover's crack. With each pass, Dakota's swollen shaft slid over his opening. Then it happened. When Ayden thought he couldn't take any more, Dakota pressed his cock inside. Ayden froze in place as the shaft sank deeper. He held his breath as Dakota's pubic hair ground against his ass.

They lay stacked on top of each other, gasping for air. Once his needs had begun to build again, Ayden pushed himself against his man. To his surprise, there was no hesitation as Dakota moved. He pulled outward until only the crown of his shaft remained inside

Ayden. He paused for an instant then sank back to his base in one long push.

Ayden shoved his face into the pillow to keep the scream of pleasure from echoing through the house. His choice proved fortunate when Dakota began fucking him like a wild man. Ayden took him again and again as his pleasure built.

With each thrust, Dakota slammed into his pleasure center, bringing him closer. Ayden writhed across the mattress, his hands clutched in tight fists. Then, with a slam that shook the massive bed, Dakota rammed himself inside Ayden. He sensed Dakota's shiver, then the first jet of his orgasm started. Dakota's climax rolled on for what seemed an eternity, although a very pleasurable one. By the time it eased to a finish, Ayden felt the beginning of his own climax approaching.

His muscles tightened, and the first round launched and landed in a white trail. His body convulsed in a slow, delightful series until the final wave of pleasure rolled through him. They writhed in the bed, holding tight against each other as they recovered.

Soon the fiery flush that had covered his body just minutes earlier began to ease. As the room cooled, Ayden curled upward, grabbed the sheet and drew it over them. He managed to keep from moaning as his lover kissed down his neck. But when Dakota pressed on his torso, Ayden grabbed his hands and kissed each palm. "Don't get anything else started. It's a miracle we didn't wake Rory."

Dakota shot him an antagonistic glance that shifted to something else. His expression seemed as if he needed to have a serious conversation.

"What?" Ayden asked.

"I don't want to cause problems, but I don't think we can both be taking a run at National Finals and still take care of Rory."

Ayden recoiled, afraid of the direction this conversation was going. He didn't want the whole newly repaired relationship to fall apart. Before he could say anything to Dakota, the cowboy continued.

"My chances are shot for this year, while you're kicking ass. What do you think about this plan? You go at the roping as hard as you can and Rory and I will stay here and take care of the ranch. Think we could make that work?"

Ayden was stunned by the change in Dakota's perspective. He'd had a complete reversal in focus from the man Ayden had walked out on. He worked to form words for how he felt, but before he could, Dakota began again. "It isn't like you'd be on your own. Rory and I would see you as often as we could. We'd be your number one cheerleaders."

Ayden's next question shot out before he considered it for too long. "What about your career?"

The reply was immediate. "It can wait, at least for this year. I'm willing to hold off that long. Then next year we can talk about it again and see what's best for all of us."

He gave Dakota a burning kiss. "Dang, you sound all mature."

Dakota considered his reply when they heard from the other room, "Daddy? Papa? Where are you?"

In the scramble that followed, their conversation came to an end. But Ayden had no intention of letting it die.

Chapter Nineteen

His horse shifted and paced as they waited for their round. Ayden would have normally tried to calm her, but being in the arena for the National Finals Rodeo put a brand-new level of tension on both of them. This was Nationals, not some small-town event where he could intimidate the other contenders. These people knew they were the best. No one would let nerves be the deciding factor.

Well, he hoped his anxiety didn't get the better of him, at least. An instant later another roper went into action and Ayden stood in his stirrups to see how they did.

The ride was short and effective as the contestant's hands flew into the air at the ride's end. It was a good run. Even worse for Ayden's ego, it was Kit. During the last few months, they had become bitter rivals. Throughout the season they had traded rankings regularly. But during the finals, he had consistently outperformed Ayden by at least a full second. The man was gnawing away at his confidence.

With his attention focused elsewhere, the mare slid sideways and pinned him against the fence. "Damn it. Knock that off!"

"You're making her nervous. She can tell you aren't under control."

He turned toward the voice to find Shane leaning against the corral panel, watching him.

Great. I didn't want this now.

"She's right too. You'd think I was some wet-behind-the-ears high school kid at his first rodeo."

At that point a noise erupted somewhere close to them and the horse bucked. "Damn! This is so fucked up. Got any suggestions?"

Shane shrugged. "Pretend this is some county fair. Your nerves are because of the stakes involved. What's the worst thing that could happen?"

"I could lose!"

"So? How much damage would that do?"

"I dunno. It would make it harder to make ends meet. Dakota would have to earn more. The ranch would become a full-time job."

"All annoying, but nothing earth-shattering. So, hold yourself together for a few more rounds. If things go bad, regroup and decide what works for your family."

"Okay, okay. I get your point. I might—and I emphasize *might*—have gotten wrapped up into today's competition."

"Maybe…but only a little." Shane replied with a smirk. "I'll head out and let you go through whatever ritual you have before a run. Dustin and I snagged two seats with Dakota and Rory."

With a backward wave, Shane disappeared into the milling crowd. Ayden stared after him for a few seconds before wrenching his attention back to the roping.

The contestant just ahead of him was preparing himself. The horse and rider were among the more nervous. The big gelding made a few abortive runs at the barrier, but the roper got the animal under control. With the last charge, they seem to have reached a level of restraint. The cowboy backed his mount into the box and a second later they erupted into the arena. The lasso toss seemed off to Ayden, but he didn't have the best vantage point.

A few quick seconds later the cowboy reached the end of the rope and the conditions didn't improve. He struggled to throw the calf, but by the end of the run, things turned to shit. The cowboy threw up his hands a few seconds later. Ayden thought the tie would hold, then the calf fought again. The tie popped loose and the calf bolted. Ayden watched, shaking his head.

Damn. That sucks.

He watched the cowboy's shoulders sag as he made his way out of the ring. The man's dejection was obvious, even from Ayden's position. He let out a sigh and patted Rose on the neck.

"Let's not have our own epic fail. I'd like to at least catch the calf."

The mare snorted and pranced before flicking her tail.

Their run was up.

Ayden guided his mount through the maze of pens, ready to enter the arena. He heard his name booming over the speaker system. The logistics of working his way through the runways registered only to a limited degree. There was an echoing roar as he entered the stadium. Rose showed off with her tail arched high and hooves prancing as they entered the box. Ayden took a moment to stand in his stirrups and wave to the crowd. The resulting cheer brought a smile to his lips.

Ayden focused on positioning Rose perfectly. Once he was happy with the setup, he gave the guy at the gate a nod. At that point, the years of practice and training kicked in. As the calf shot out, Rose contracted like a coiled spring and exploded to chase it down. Her massive hindquarters shot them into action.

She was in pursuit of the calf, sprinting across the powder fine arena floor like a West Texas jack rabbit. Ayden's heart pounded in his ears as he flipped the noose and released its stiff circumference at the escaping calf. The instant he threw the lasso, the mare slammed onto her rump and Ayden launched himself down the rope. The rigid lariat yanked the calf into a back flip. Ayden raced to it, timing perfectly to bring it under his control and tie the struggling animal with the short length of rope he carried between his teeth for that purpose.

He finished and threw his hands into the air. The millisecond he did, the timer sounded. With his round ended, he walked back to Rose, who was still working her way backward to keep the calf under control. He released the animal and recoiled his lasso. Then in a long-practiced motion, Ayden mounted his horse and loped her out of the arena.

As he left, he plucked his hat off and waved it at the audience. The roar that resulted brought a smile to his lips. A satisfactory round and a pumped crowd — what more could a cowboy want?

The exit gate opened and a flush of happiness washed through Ayden. Dakota stood just inside the alleyway holding Rory on one hip. When he got closer, he realized Rory was bouncing up and down, yelling at the top of his lungs.

"Papa! Papa! You won. You're the champion."

Dakota gave Ayden a peck on the cheek and beamed at him. Before he could ask, he got an update on his standing.

"It's close, but Kit has his last round to run. It would take a miracle for him to pull it out of his butt."

Ayden gave a nod then beamed at his family. "We're going to win this thing. We'll take the whole shooting match."

"Your round was amazing," Dakota said. "I don't see how you could have made it any faster."

Rose pranced in place as the nervous energy affected her. After fighting her for a few moments, he turned to Dakota.

"She's getting wound up. I'll run her to the trailer while you guys go back to your seats. In a few minutes the whole thing ends, and we can celebrate."

"Oh, we're going to party, something you'd only dreamed of in Vegas."

Ayden chuckled and guided Rose through the crowd. He reached his destination in time to hear the audience groan. *At least that tells me the next cowboy missed his calf.* He settled Rose into her stall and headed back to the stadium at a run. He popped out of the entry closest to where his family was watching the event. Dakota spotted him and motioned toward them.

"Hurry! Kit's next and is in the arena."

Ayden scrambled down the row of seats until he reached Dakota and Rory. When he gazed around, he caught the smiling face of Dakota's mother. He gave her a wave before taking Rory and settling on the bench. They were seated just as Kit backed his mount into the box. Ayden could almost sense everything clicking into place, and a heartbeat later, Kit gave a quick nod.

The calf exploded from the chute as a blur. As Ayden's focus shifted to the rider, his horse coiled so it was almost bent double. The sprint ended an instant later when Kit released his lasso. The stiff lariat shot out like a striking rattler, settling into place as the horse skidded to a stop.

Kit flew from his mount and ran down the taut lasso to the struggling calf. The next seconds ticked off as the pigging rope flew into place. The bound calf hit the ground as Kit threw his hands into the air and the stop-clock sounded.

For Ayden, the world compressed into the next few seconds that ended when they posted Kit's time. It would be close, because his run had been under eight seconds. Kit needed a great performance to win. Then the announcer's voice ground out the results of this round and the overall scores from all ten days.

Ayden watched the scoreboard with growing apprehension. Dakota slipped his hand to the back of his neck and gave a supportive squeeze. Then the results appeared over the board. Seconds ticked past until only the top two slots remained unassigned.

"Ah, shit."

He took an instant to realize the source of the statement, and it wasn't Dakota. Then he spent a minute keeping from laughing at their son and controlling his disappointment.

"Rory!"

"Sorry, Papa. You should have won."

Dakota drew him into a tight hug then released him with a quick kiss. "Second place at the National Finals is darn good."

Ayden gave himself a few seconds to gather his thoughts before he spoke. "I would have loved to beat Kit's ass, but it didn't happen. We'll take a few days off before planning next year. It's all good."

"Regardless, we're going out to celebrate. This is a great year. We're all together and my boyfriend almost won the tie-down roping at the National Finals Rodeo. Those are all great things. You get to pick where you'd like to go."

A shy grin crept across Ayden's face. "Well, if I get to pick..."

"Yup. Whatever you want."

"I've heard Cleaver is fantastic."

"Done!" Dakota said.

* * * *

Dakota let his gaze travel around the room and tried not to be overwhelmed. He was pleased to have snagged a table at one of the more exclusive steakhouses in Vegas. They'd only been seated for a few minutes and were already enjoying a great glass of cold beer.

"Nice choice, son. I can't remember the last time I ate at a restaurant this upscale. Thank you for inviting me to join you."

Dakota smiled at his mother as he took another sip. The dark liquid was one of the best microbrews he'd ever had.

"I thought it would be an event to share."

The table went quiet as everyone, including Rory, admired the surroundings. A short time later the appetizers arrived and they began enjoying what Dakota hoped would be the most memorable night of their lives. A familiar deep voice brought him back to the present.

"Congratulations, Ayden. Nice set of runs this year," Shane said.

It pleased Dakota to see the man who'd bred and trained Ayden's horse standing beside them with his husband. They both seemed happy with themselves. Shane hesitated until Dustin took over the conversation.

"Ayden, we'd like to sponsor you for next season. Our horses are in demand because of how you performed on Rose. We've already had several ropers interested in looking over a few of last year's fillies."

Pride grew in Dakota at the offer they'd made to his lover, and from the expression on Ayden's face, the answer would be yes. Once Ayden could keep the tears under control, he nodded and choked out a reply.

"Yes. I'd love that, either with Rose or a new horse—whatever you think would work best for you."

Shane smiled. "Once you recover, we can work out the details. We'll get you an amazing mount."

A moment passed then Dustin took Shane by the arm. "Shane, we've taken enough of these fine folks' time. I know how you are about making battle strategies, so I won't let us stick around."

Before Dakota could say anything, Ayden chimed into the discussion. "No, stay and celebrate with us." He turned to Dakota. "You don't mind, do you?"

Dakota saw his plans crumbling away. He rebounded and decided his scheme might change, but everything was to the good. "Sure! Everyone is welcome. No one will ever forget tonight."

Dustin studied the group for a minute before shrugging. "I have a feeling I will regret this. Okay, but I insist Shane and I pay for our own meals."

Dakota agreed, and within a few minutes, the newcomers were nursing drinks. It was the most comfortable conversation he'd had in a long time. He liked getting the opportunity to know Shane and Dustin better. The waiter cleared the empty dishes then came back, smiling at Dakota.

"I was told this table had a specific dessert."

Dakota's excitement had built for the last few minutes and now his emotions threatened to burst. Glances of confusion flew as their waiter returned and trailing behind him was a young cowboy carrying an acoustic guitar.

By the time they reached the table, Ayden was shaking. The young man swung the instrument into place and struck a chord. He then flashed them a brilliant smile. "This is for Ayden from Dakota."

Ayden slapped his hands over his mouth as he played. He had barely finished the first chorus when Ayden wiped his eyes and croaked out. "It's *Amazed*. Oh my God."

For the rest of the song, their table was silent except for the occasional sniffle. Conversation ended around them, but Dakota focused on Ayden, who was crying a torrent. As the song eased to its conclusion, the room became silent.

Ayden turned to him and Dakota pulled a box from his pocket then dropped to one knee. With his own tears flowing, Dakota opened the container and held the ring between his fingers.

"Ayden, I can't imagine spending the rest of my life with anyone else. You're always there for me. I want to make it official. Ayden Haskell, would you marry me?"

Ayden sobbed and wiped his nose on a napkin Dakota had handed him. He lifted Dakota to his feet and gave him a heated kiss.

"Yes, of course I will!" Ayden shouted.

The room erupted with noises of every type as the people trumpeted their approval.

Chapter Twenty

Sheer curtains billowed into the room, waking Dakota to the bloom of the day in the Keys. He slipped from where he'd curled against Ayden and padded to the glass balcony doors. His cock hung full and heavy from the activities of the previous night. Their wedding had left Dakota with enough memories for a lifetime. The party had lasted long into the night and its culmination had him and his new husband feeling like the luckiest people in the world.

Enjoying the late-morning air, Dakota held the curtain open a crack to relish the sight of the turquoise water surrounding tiny Duck Key, where the resort was nestled. A cool breeze blew from the ocean sending him back to the king-size bed to cuddle.

Ayden slipped his hands over Dakota's waist and pulled them together. The heat of their joined bodies traveled through him as Ayden kissed the side of his neck. Dakota responded to the attention until his cock was hard as concrete. He turned slowly, wrapped his hand around their combined dicks and stroked them.

The delicious sensation built in ways Dakota wouldn't have expected in such a short time. And judging from the sounds Ayden was making, his efforts were having their desired effects as well.

He twisted each hard nipple until a stream of whimpers filled the entire room. Dakota slipped in close and gnawed on each one until they flushed a deep red.

"Fuck, Dakota. That's so good."

"If you think that's good, just wait."

He sank between his man's spread legs.

Ayden shivered when Dakota wrapped his mouth around his cock. He grabbed Dakota's shoulders and moaned. "Oh shit, babe. That's fucking amazing."

He let Ayden's shaft slip out then licked it like adult candy. When he drove his tongue into Ayden's slit, his husband trembled. At that point, Dakota started his way back up Ayden's naked body until he pressed his lips to Ayden's. Dakota pinned him against the mattress, pouring all of his passion into the kiss.

Dakota vaulted from the bed and smirked as he walked to their bags and found the bottle of lube he'd packed. He returned, crawled beside Ayden and teased him with it.

"What should I do with this? 'Cause I have a few ideas."

Ayden stroked his hard dick while he gave Dakota a hungry gaze. "Get me good and slick. I'm wanting some of what you're selling."

Dakota squirted a strand of lube down the underside of Ayden's swollen shaft. He wrapped his fingers around its thickness and had Ayden squirming as he teased its length. His eyes were closed and his mouth gaping as Dakota pleasured him.

Dakota gathered lube across two fingers and began getting himself ready. He worked the gel deeper, adding more when needed until he buried his fingers knuckle deep in his own ass. Seconds later, Dakota slid across Ayden, trapping Ayden's dick between his ass cheeks. Dakota rocked back and forth, adding Ayden's abundant precum to his slick hole. When Dakota couldn't wait any longer, he trapped the head of Ayden's dick against him and pushed.

Dakota's ass stretched as Ayden entered him. The ripples of pain and pleasure built as he moved, opening himself more with each pass. Then it happened... Dakota widened the final bit needed and Ayden slid inside.

"Ah, fuck. Wait a second. You're thick. Give me a chance to get used to you," Dakota said.

Ayden rubbed his hands across Dakota's chest and worked his hard nipples. Intense pleasure flowed through Dakota for several minutes, then he sank deeper, sliding in until he ground against Ayden's bush.

"Fuck," Dakota sighed.

"Yeah, this is sweet," Ayden agreed.

Dakota leaned forward, placing his hands on Ayden's chest and stroking over it as he slid back and forth. It didn't take long before sexual desire was cresting in Dakota. Too soon, Dakota sensed the familiar euphoria of his impending orgasm.

"Ayden. Too early. Not ready," Dakota warned.

"Turn over. I want to plow your ass."

It took a second for the request to register with Dakota, but when it did, he gave a huge grin.

Ayden pulled out and Dakota climbed to his hands and knees. He glanced back in time to see the expression on Aiden's face as he slapped one of Dakota's ass cheeks while pressing his shaft against Dakota's ready hole. He groaned at the stinging intrusion, but the blend of pain and pleasure crested in multiple waves that had Dakota on the edge. A final sensation that sent him over the top was when Ayden reached between his legs and stroked his hard cock.

Desire sent him into an uncontrollable spiral of hedonistic pleasure. Seconds later, Dakota's body tensed. He trembled for a moment before the first strand of cum shot from his cock and across the bedding. Two more followed in quick succession and had Dakota trembling. His pleasure peaked again and again, leaving a thick white strand each time. The final spasm racked his body and, with a rattling moan, Dakota sighed and collapsed with Ayden wedged inside him.

Ayden paused for an instant then resumed thrusting. With Dakota pinned to the bed, Ayden fucked him like a madman. Dakota recognized Ayden was close. He'd reach his orgasm in a matter of seconds.

"Fuck me, stud. Fill my ass," Dakota said in encouragement.

Ayden grabbed Dakota's hips and buried his cock inside as his climax began. With each shudder, Dakota took in more cum. Once Ayden had given Dakota everything he had, he fell across him, kissed the side of his neck then whispered, "Oh my God, that was amazing. I don't think I'll be able to move for a week."

Dakota rolled until they lay facing each other. He kissed Ayden and drew his fingertips over his cheek. "I love you above everything else. The rest is gravy."

Ayden chuckled and gave Dakota a peck on the forehead. "You have the strangest sayings, almost as bad as someone from Oklahoma." His expression grew serious. "I love you too. I can't wait to share our lives."

Dakota nodded and kissed him again. Rory came to his thoughts. "When we get back home, we need to make Rory your kid too. I want to minimize the crap if something happens."

Ayden curled beside Dakota, resting a cheek on his shoulder. "Let's hope hard times are over. I think we've earned a break for a while."

They lay without talking, serenaded by the sounds of the gulls above the marina. Then Ayden popped up.

"Where is our son?"

Dakota chuckled. "He's with his grandmother. She volunteered to keep him last night. I saw them just before she took him upstairs, and Rory was negotiating sugar cookies and wedding cake for breakfast."

Ayden chuckled and rolled to the edge of the bed. He stood with a bounce then reached back for Dakota and led him to the shower.

"Come on. We can clean up and meet your mother. Otherwise, she'll hunt us down."

They had taken only a few steps when Dakota's phone rang. He eyed Ayden then let out a roaring laugh and motioned toward the phone.

"I'm not looking!"

Dakota sprinted the rest of the way to the bathroom while Ayden followed behind, shaking his head.

Want to see more from this author?
Here's a taster for you to enjoy!

Tackling the Subject
Jon Keys

Excerpt

A shaft of light landed on the thick red hair covering Sam's forearm. He shifted a little deeper into the tomb-quiet, cavernous room. The rows and rows of books in their order and symmetry had always comforted him — just like writing code for new software, which he was kick ass at doing. There should be logic to biology, too. It might not be obvious, but somewhere in all that squishiness it had order. Sam liked things that had order.

He glanced at the screen of his computer. No new mail. Their appointment was at three. Not three-o-five. Sam was already angry that he'd had to ask for a tutor. Well, really more embarrassed that some whiz kid had to explain the confusing field of biology. Sam resented the hell out of it. *Mutation?* Computers didn't mutate. Code didn't mutate. It was driving him crazy.

He glanced at his watch again. Two more minutes. He sighed and reminded himself that he had to pass this class. It was one of those courses he'd had to take outside his major. *If I wanted to know about meiosis and mitosis, then I'd take the class on my own. But the university thinks I need to be educated about crap I don't care about.*

The air conditioner came on and a shaft of cool air blew across him. It carried an almost antiseptic tang along with the faint musty scent of books printed before his grandparents' time. He glanced at the screen on his watch. *Another minute and he'll be late. It figures.*

Sam stretched his long legs, letting his flip-flops dangle from his bare toes. He realized someone had invaded his part of the library's fifth floor. His frown deepened when he recognized it was one of the brainless hulks from the football team. Sam tensed as the lumbering brute moved closer. *Go away. Go back to your cave and leave normal people alone.*

His discomfort level grew as the guy walked toward him. *Short dark hair, western shirt, jeans and boots. Well, he's at the right university.* Their distance narrowed and Sam dropped his gaze in the hope he would pass without stopping. His nervousness built until, by the time they were side by side, there was a slight tremble going through his body and bile in his mouth. Triggers from years past fired like a cheap six-gun. He tensed even further when the guy stopped beside him. Sam was angry and his appraisal turned into a glare he shot at the lummox. But before he said anything, he heard.

"Are you Samuel Doherty?"

At first, it startled Sam that the guy had his name. But his rancor flared when he realized the man was reading it from a card and held a copy of his biology textbook under one arm. *This is my tutor? It's bad enough I need help at all. This makes it insulting.* He looked up and scowled. "Yes, I'm Sam."

"Cool. I'm Gordy, your biology tutor."

Sam sat stunned, staring in disbelief at the person they'd sent. Without considering the consequences, he blurted out. "Wasn't there anyone else?"

Gordy lifted an eyebrow and gave him a quiet expression of disapproval. "I aced the class you're failing, so I'm quite capable of helping you. But it's up to you if you want my assistance or not."

Sam sat without moving then realized the jock— *What's his name? Gordy?* —was still waiting for an answer. Just getting help from one of the university jock squad had his muscles taut with anger and distaste. But the midterm was coming, and he had to pass this class. If this was who the Help Center had assigned him, then he was capable of helping Sam. But with feelings approaching hatred, Sam didn't understand how he would get the assistance he needed from Gordy. *It had to be a damn football player?*

"I can go if you want. I had to rearrange everything to meet with you today, so..." Gordy said.

Sam swallowed hard. *I have to suppress my feelings. I don't know him. He might be a good guy. I suppose that's possible. That's one of the goals from the therapist. That I shouldn't paint everyone with the same broad strokes.* Gordy frowned and turned to go, leaving Sam to his private corner.

"Hang on. Yeah, I need help. Damn biology."

Gordy rounded the table and stopped opposite Sam. They studied each other for a long minute before Gordy took the last steps and sat beside him. Sam's nose wrinkled. Gordy had the faint scent of sweat, bringing back those awful, secret memories. He had to fight the urge to put his hand over his nose to lessen the odor.

"You're in Bio 101, right?" Gordy asked.

Sam pulled his sleeve down his arm and pressed his nose against it. Gordy's funk was all he could think about.

"Yeah, Bio 101 with Hawthorne."

"The labs or the lectures?"

"Both. Some of it I don't get." Sam considered for a minute. "Actually, I don't get most of it. It isn't logical."

Gordy stopped flipping through the textbook and studied Sam. "It is logical. It all follows patterns and systems. What's your major?"

"Computer science. You can't get more structured than that. It's all ones and zeros. I understand it well enough that campus IT hired me."

"Biology is all made of elements. From there, you get molecules and everything else. That's basic."

Sam ground his teeth, losing his nonexistent patience with his overrated tutor. Gordy's odor had expanded and had become a distinctive metallic note on the back of his tongue.

"Okay. According to Dr. Hawthorne's syllabus, you're at the part of the textbook covering cell division. Does that seem about right?"

He slid the opened textbook over to Sam and leaned closer to check the information at the beginning of the chapter. The odor strengthened and the heat coming from Gordy's body was obvious. Sam scrubbed his knuckles across his nose, becoming more frustrated with each passing moment.

Gordy bounced his leg as he explained a particular part of the complicated heredity equation, which Sam understood none of.

"Are you getting this? It's confusing. A lot of people have trouble understanding how it works."

Sam's anger flared again, but he calmed himself. "Yeah, it's not bad. The cells split, the chromosomes split, everything splits. But it's so boring. How do you keep it all in your head?"

Gordy considered him for a moment. "You get the numbers, then. Do the structures make sense to you? Are you having trouble remembering the details?"

Sam knew his face must be bright red. This jock wasn't going to talk to him as if he was a fifth grader. He decided the time had come for him to let Gordy understand how he felt. "Look. I'm good at my major and can remember several computer languages. I wouldn't be taking this stupid biology class if I didn't have to so I can graduate. And what I don't need is attitude from a damn jock."

Gordy pushed away from the table and his shirt billowed then fell against his chest, filling the surrounding air with the musky scent Sam found so offensive. That was the last straw. He lost what tiny amount of decorum he had.

"Oh my God, you stink. You smell like a goat or something. Don't you ever shower?"

Gordy stared at Sam until the tension between them was palpable. His heavy eyebrows twisted together until the space between them almost disappeared. A muscle in his jaw knotted and unknotted so fast that it seemed to jump. His lips pressed together hard until all that remained was a tight slash across his lower face. Gordy dragged the textbook back and it was obvious that only strength of will allowed him to close the book with just a soft thud. He tucked the tome under his arm and started down the aisle.

"That's it? The whiz kid of biology is running off without doing his job? Isn't that just typical? Well, run, Mister Football Stud, and take the funky locker room stink with you."

Gordy stopped, his muscles tensing as he drew in a breath and held it for a minute before turning to Sam. He stalked closer, leaning into Sam until their faces were inches apart. Light flashed across his deep brown eyes, and the amber filigree that surrounded the iris seemed to be molten lava. Sam recognized a trace of mint on Gordy's breath as they glared at each other.

Gordy bit off his first words. "So, you think I stink? Some of us don't have everything handed to us. We have to work to pay for school. You're the one who whined to Connie in the Help Center and said you had to get help *today*. I rearranged my schedule, did my workout early to shower and get here on time. And what you smell is soap. I don't know what your problem is, but it started long before I got here."

Rage, indignation and a slight amount of fear coursed through Sam as he stared at the big linebacker. He refused to let himself be intimidated by their differences in size. He'd never let someone bully him again. "I thought you could be professional and do your job. But I guess if it's not football, you don't give a fuck about it. I'm sure you're already getting paid for this session, so why don't you shuffle off to meet with your no-neck Neanderthal buddies to talk about trying to intimidate the person who paid you to help them."

Gordy's jaw clamped down hard and the bouncing jaw muscle became a fixed point. "Before I lose what little cool I still have left, I'm leaving, but you're an ass."

"At least I'm not a mindless thug who picks on people smaller than them and enjoys it."

Gordy grabbed his bulging backpack and tossed it over his shoulder as if it were weightless. He turned to Sam again. His expression contained more pity. "You have issues. You should get help."

Rage flared in Sam as Gordy turned and made his way off the floor.

"Wait a minute!" Sam yelled.

"Hey. Keep it down. I'm trying to study for a chem test and I can't concentrate."

Sam glanced in time to see the person who had scolded him disappear behind his desk. By the time he turned back, Gordy was gone.

Sam ground his teeth as he gathered his bag. He would pass this class, and he didn't need the help from a muscle-bound jock.

* * * *

Gordy tried to focus on helping Sarah with the tamales she was making. He'd worked for weeks talking her into making a batch of the labor-intensive treats. He'd eaten them before at various Mexican restaurants but had never been impressed. Then his best friend Nate'd had him over to try the version his then-girlfriend made. They had been delicious. Since then, he'd nagged Sarah constantly for more of the cornhusk-wrapped delicacies.

Sarah peered over his shoulder. "I don't want it too hot. Just melt the lard and it makes it easier to stir with the masa. It's one of the tricks of my tamales."

Gordy stirred the contents of the saucepan carefully before he shot Sarah a grin. "Are you kidding? I've been trying to get you to make more tamales since yours and Nate's wedding. I'm planning to do exactly what you tell me to do" — Gordy's expression tightened — "unlike the idiot who signed up for tutoring today. He was an ass."

"Gordon Hager, watch your mouth," Sarah scolded him.

Gordy rolled his eyes at Nate but apologized. "Sorry, Sarah, but he was. He said I stunk and that I was an ignorant jock. I'll have him know that I'd just showered before going to the library. And it wasn't like I asked him to meet on Sunday. Pis..." He glanced at Sarah as she shredded the pork. "Pulling something like that ticks me off."

"What was his major?"

"Computer science. He said biology didn't make sense."

Nate chuckled as he ate one of the cookies Sarah had made. "The whole school thing isn't as easy for some of us as it is for you."

Gordy rolled his eyes but kept his mouth shut. He concentrated on filling the tamales, folding them and stacking them in the steamer. When the first layer was finished, she turned to Gordy with a smile.

"He was cute, wasn't he? You thought he was cute."

Gordy frowned at her. "That had nothing to do with it. He was such a jerk. It was unbelievable."

Sarah carefully spread a layer of the tamale dough over the cornhusk and handed it to Gordy. After a few minutes passed, Sarah began to talk. "What's he look like?"

Gordy refused to meet her gaze. "I don't know. About my height. Skinny. You know, typical college guy."

Nate came around the counter to help fit the last of the tamales into the steamer. They finished the final layer, put on the lid then Nate carried it to the stove. He turned and wrapped his arms around Sarah and grinned at Gordy. As always, Gordy couldn't keep from thinking what a beautiful couple they made. Nate's muscular body and mahogany coloring were the perfect foil for Sarah's bright red curls and porcelain skin. He started to mention to them again about what a good-looking couple they made, but Nate waved dismissively.

"Stop stalling. What aren't you telling us? You're avoiding the questions more than I did when I was telling my mother I'd proposed to Sarah."

"And how did that go?"

Nate grinned. "We're married. She speaks to us. If we ever have kids, she'll be happier, but then she's that way with my brothers and sisters. And we did go through the whole marriage thing."

"Good information, even if I think my parents will implode when they find out their oldest son likes dudes."

"They did fine when they met your black roommate. Give them a little slack. But you're stalling. What is it about difficult-tutor-boy that makes you grin every time you talk about him?"

Sarah cocked an eyebrow and joined Nate in their showdown. But it didn't take long for Gordy to give in after Sarah glanced over to the tamales with a significant expression.

"All right, fine. You don't have to threaten with the tamales. He's cute, okay? As tall as I am but with a runner's build. There's also an adorable sprinkling of freckles across the bridge of his nose. He's my type in just about every way."

Nate started to ask more questions, but Gordy interrupted him. "Okay, fine. Jeez! He has the sexiest dark-auburn hair. But it doesn't matter how good-looking he is, he was a jerk and I'm not dealing with him again."

By now, Gordy was getting frustrated with his friends, and he thought they were aware of it, too, since the conversation slipped away from his personal life to the safer topics of food and football.

By the time Gordy gathered up his gear to head home, he was stuffed with tamales and had enough in freezer bags to last him for several meals. He pulled his boots on just as Sarah stepped closer and he gave her his usual hug. "Thanks for inviting me over. As always, everything was delicious."

She whispered in his ear before letting him go, "Don't worry about the cute guy. The right man will come along."

Gordy kept his thoughts to himself and gave her a final tight hug.

"Gorrrdeeee!"

Gordy's grin was genuine as he and Nate jumped at each other. Their chest bump rattled the dishes drying in the sink and sent each of them backward for several feet.

"Boys!" Sarah muttered.

PUBLISHING

Sign up for our newsletter and find out about all our
romance book releases, eBook sales and promotions,
sneak peeks and FREE romance books!

About the Author

Jon Keys' earliest memories revolve around books; with the first ones he can recall reading himself being "The Warlord of Mars" and anything with Tarzan. (The local library wasn't particularly up to date.) But as puberty set in, he started sneaking his mother's romance magazines and added the world of romance and erotica to his mix of science fiction, fantasy, Native American, westerns and comic books.

A voracious reader for almost half a century, Jon has only recently begun creating his own flights of fiction for the entertainment of others. Born in the Southwest and now living in the Midwest, Jon has worked as a ranch hand, teacher, computer tech, roughneck, designer, retail clerk, welder, artist, and, yes, pool boy; with interests ranging from kayaking and hunting to painting and cooking, he draws from a wide range of life experiences to create written works that draw the reader in and wrap them in a good story.

Jon loves to hear from readers. You can find his contact information, website details and author profile page at https://www.pride-publishing.com